A Teenager's Ambitions

Romance

Teenager's Ambitions

Abdenal Carvalho

SUMMARY

First Chapter - Poverty

It was a family from the periphery, similar to all others with its social and economic difficulties that prevented it from boasting luxury and wealth. The daily life of its members was based on the need for everything, which caused hopelessness in some and outrage in others. This was the case with Nathalia, a teenager who was completely embittered by the poverty that surrounded her on all sides.

— Damn it! Mother, did you see that jeans shorts I got as a gift from Aunt Marta?

— How do I know if I'm not using it?

— Nice answer, it helped a lot! And now, where did that crap go? Chris, did you see my Jeans shorts?!

— It must be in the laundry basket, little princess. You're the type to never wash the clothes you wear!

— What a big crap! And now, what am I going to use to go talk to that fret, is it the best outfit I have?

— Go naked, he will surely love it!

— Fuck you, disgusting tomboy!

As in most suburban homes, communication between family members was sparse with kindness, always done with great harshness. Nathalia do Valle was as beautiful as her name suggests, conveying the idea of fame and power, however, she was just a teenager who was not satisfied with her reality.

It was her mother who chose to give her that name, taken from a famous actress from the soap operas she used to watch on television. Perhaps that is why the girl brought so much pride and arrogance within her, it was as if she were not part of that miserable world in which she was born.

— Are you going to find that white boy from school?

— That white boy has a name, you see, and lots of money!

— And does he have any idea how poor you are?

— Look here, girl, it will hurt you!

— My sister, you're still going to be very bad at living trying to hit these cool guys

— Stay at yours, Chris, don't get into big people. Go study your books and see if you leave my life alone. Ah, lend me those sneakers that Daddy gave you as a gift, mine took the bran a long time ago

— Ah, am I useful now?

— You know what, oh little hollow stick, give me the damn thing about that shoe and stay there with your face buried in the notebooks that I have more to do!

There was a huge contrast between those two sisters, a visible difference.

While Christina was passionate about her studies and fought for a promising future, Nathalia was totally the opposite, she dreamed of a life made of greatness and power, however, she sought it in an obscure, erroneous, misleading and disloyal way.

Although his purposes were good, his attitudes were bad. She wanted at all costs to become rich, important and stay forever away from the humble origin for which she felt so much contempt. He thought of living in the comfort of a good home, having all the money he needed to buy everything he could never have before, being different, running away from that tacky family with whom he lived all his childhood and adolescence.

— Wow, what a delay!

— Sorry, princess, I had some setbacks

— Good thing it comes by car because if it was by bus it would take a century to get here and I would not waste any more time, waiting

— Stop being angry, I'm already here, right?

— Where are you taking me? Aren't we going back to that damn zoo? I'm tired of seeing those filthy bugs every Sunday

— Angry girl, you, huh?

— You're too slow to count!

— Look here, if you're complaining that until now, I didn't take you to meet my parents, I'm sorry to tell you it's not my fault, they are very busy

— Okay, so let's go to the zoo every weekend to see smelly animals? What the fuck!

— No. Today we go to the cinema

She was not born with the capacity to love, she saw this feeling with contempt and made fun of seeing people in love. Their purpose in dating that rich young man was simply in order that they could get married and secure the future. After all, he was the only heir to a great fortune.

He would become the owner of all the family's assets after his father's death, a great businessman with an important name in the business world. His ambition was limitless. Thanks to the extreme beauty that was peculiar to him, he ended up winning the heart of Vinicius, who even belonging to Elite studied at the same school as her, at a time when the public school.

System in this country was more respected than the private one. However, the contrast between the two was visible. For if on the one hand he tried to live a great love story, on the other she just wanted to take advantage of that relationship

— You bring me to the damn cinema and you don't even let me see the movie, you kept kissing me all the time!

— But that was my plan, to kiss in the dark of the cinema

— Plan ova, if you wanted to keep kneading me, we should go to the motel right away!

— Here you come again with this chat

— Come here, Dude, are you gay by any chance? Gosh, all my friends are having sex only, I'm stranded!

— Sometimes I wonder how a girl your age lives inviting her boyfriend to have sex, when the obvious would be that I would make this proposal to you.

— True, it's really strange that the guy I date is so soft!

— You do not exist...

— You know what, leave me there on my street, which is better, I saw that there is no rabbit coming out of this bush!

While Nathalia was rude and expressed herself only by shouting, Vinicius Sales was a methodical, respectful young man, focused on the principles inherited from the education received from his parents, belonging to an orthodox Christian family, from those who teach their children the opposite of what other young people live there. Outside.

 Like sexual freedom and the unthinkable attitudes characteristic of youth without restraint. He had as a rule the commitment to the sanctity of the body, never practicing sex outside of marriage. She had a deep understanding of the matter, as her aunt Marta was an evangelical and explained the details of the religion.

Thus, she kept urging her boyfriend to go to bed in order to be able to get pregnant and force a more serious commitment. He understood that because he was a defender of moral concepts, he would never abandon a woman pregnant with his child. But to his discontent he refused to give in to his insistent pleas.

There were times when he lacked patience when he had to deal with such slowness, that he didn't act like a real male, getting to the point. However, expectations about this would be far from being fulfilled, as the boy was completely averse to the practice of sex irresponsibly.

- Um, in a big car with a fancy boyfriend, huh?

— Take your eye off, neighbor, envy kills!

— I don't know, Pedro, but this is going to be the shame of this family, it looks like they're going to be a whore. If not already!

— Is that any of your business, woman? Go worry about our daughter, that's right!

— Hey, up there, see? My Brenda is a golden girl, she lives with her face buried in books and will still make us very proud. It's far from looking like this one, God forbid!

Living in a poor neighborhood, located on the outskirts of the city and suddenly appearing accompanied by a nigger, parading in a car of the year, he couldn't help but fall into the mouth of the gossips on duty, earning the title of prostitute.

— So, how about the date?

— A terrible drug!

— Mercy, but nothing good in this life for you, my sister?

— And is it my fault if things never work out for me, Chris?

— Don't talk nonsense, where is there another girl your age who is lucky enough to date a boy from a rich family like that?

— Tremendous softie, that's it. I don't think I'll ever meet your parents!

Days after that conversation, the seventh month of that year was approaching, a period when they would go on vacation and a trip to the interior would be ideal to escape the routine of urban centers, as usual, the boy would have to accompany his family. And would be the ideal time to introduce his new girlfriend to his parents.

However, he feared that she would not be easily accepted, since she was of a lower social level than his.

— And will he take you along on this tour?

— Of course, you silly, why wouldn't you take it?

— Hey, wake up woman, you're just a slum!

— No need to humiliate, see?

— That is not my intention, but facing reality from time to time avoids certain disappointments, that boy is in love with your physical beauty without taking into account the social difference that exists between you, my sister, but do not be deceived as to what it may happen after it is revealed to his parents

— From what he told me, his family is evangelical and without prejudice as to the social difference of people. So, I think they will accept me in a good way

— My dear sister, a man's heart can be won with a beautiful little body, but his family will not be influenced by his angel face

— Damn it, Chris, give it a try instead of being against it!

— Sorry if I look too pessimistic, it turns out I don't believe in fairy tales, I have my head in place and my feet on the ground

Me, huh, go over there, vulture!

There was no point in trying to change Nathalia's way of thinking and acting. The teenager was really determined to realize her ambition and become a very influential woman in the society of her time. As he did not have a splendid cradle, he looked for this possibility in Vinicius.

Of course not being foolish enough not to notice the immense gap between her and the reality in which she found herself, her boyfriend came from an extremely high social base in relation to her, but he had an asset in his hands, he had fallen on all fours of its immense beauty and in a short time it would no longer be necessary to be collecting coins at home to buy a hamburger in your Uncle Chico's snack car, at the beginning of the street.

— Dad, give me some change to have lunch with your uncle!

— But that's it every day, my daughter, didn't you eat anything today?

— I had lunch, but I don't want dinner, it's always the same!

— This one has a spirit of greatness, father, only likes what is good

— You'll die there, Chris!

— Stop this little haze right now!

— It is this intellectual who never tires of picking on me!

— There, you thick, can you speak a little quieter? Just know how to express yourself by screaming

— It will hurt you, I speak as you want!

— I already told the two to stop this fight!

— We are not fighting, mother, is that Nathalia can only scream

— Whatever, stop it right now! And you, man, stay there in the middle of this quiet confusion and it doesn't even serve to tell the two to shut up?

— I said, but they never hear me ...

— He said nothing, he looks like the living dead!

Useless little man, the one I married!

— Don't talk about Dad like that, Mom!

— Defend him because he keeps buying you with these change

— Stop it, woman, nothing to do! And then old man, are you going to buy me a snack or not?

— Alright, come on

Carlos was a calm man his inertia was such that he was too lazy to speak. Luiza, the wife, used to say that they only started dating and got married because she took all the necessary initiatives, otherwise nothing would have happened. He had a good appearance, he was a husband and father present, loving, attentive and he knew how to listen to everyone who sought him out.

Perhaps because of these qualities he won the love and attention of the family he formed, despite the inevitable poverty in which they lived. Each of her children inherited part of their characteristics: Nathalia, despite having a greater resemblance to her mother when speaking screaming, being ambitious and doing everything with a view to her own benefit, brought her father's determination, never giving up on her purposes.

Cristina stayed with a large part of the intelligence, because he was a man with several professional attributes, he exercised several professions that allowed him to never be unemployed, despite always earning little in exchange for his efforts. Nathan, the youngest son, learned the craft of mechanics at an early age and at the age of sixteen he already worked in the workshop of Mr. João, a well-known mechanic in the neighborhood. That evening, as usual, father and daughter went to lunch together. Put the news of the day in days.

Nathalia was completely free to open up and reveal to Carlos everything that was living in her insistent mission to get along in life, despite sometimes having to listen to certain sermons for her own good

— I am not against your desire to improve your life, my daughter, I even agree that you try to get out of this slump in which we find ourselves and change for the better, because evolving is always very good, but with certain measures in everything we do

— What do you mean, Dad?

— Never take a step beyond the size of your leg, that is, planning every detail of our actions before making certain decisions is essential for us to be victorious

— Got it

— There is a great chasm between us and our dreams, it will not always be easy to cross the river of obstacles that separate us from our goals without first running the risk of drowning and it is exactly at this crucial moment that we must be prepared not to be shipwrecked and arrive integers on the other side

— And what can we do to avoid this shipwreck?

— Be very careful! Never take any chances beyond the ability to overcome each situation, which will certainly arise during your walk

— And how do I know if I will be ready to understand all these things, before confronting them in the future?

— A very intelligent question, my girl, is where maturity in everything you decide to do will be of great importance, and how to mature in life, when we are just teenagers, we know nothing about tomorrow.

Knowing how to listen and being humble to put into practice everything that the most experienced teach us is the first step.

— Wow, Dad, how smart you are! I'm very proud to be your daughter

— First and most important lesson for your journey towards the future that awaits you, my little one, never admire the qualities of others. Rather, seek to know your own qualities deeply and try to put them into practice. Do not waste time in life, admiring the importance of other people, but strive to express yours and instead of being a fan of someone, win your own followers

— Wow, old man, how much wisdom!

— What did I just teach you? Stop admiring others' qualities and start exploring yours!

— That's right. Dad, I'll start doing this!

— So, start now, from that moment

— OK I will do it!

— So, Carlos, how are things going?

— The same routine as always ...

The two brothers started talking about their limited lives while the teenager sat at the table, enjoying a delicious snack, taking the opportunity to reflect on her father's words.

Considering all the teaching I learned from him that early evening. It was, without a shadow of a doubt, a great privilege to be the daughter of a man with such knowledge, he could not stand the mediocre existence he seemed to be resigned to, as well as all the rest of his family.

But he admired him for all he was able to teach him.

— Dad, come on!

— Yes, my angel

— My blessing, uncle!

— God bless you, princess, see you tomorrow

The days passed and Nathalia soul was distressed when she realized that nothing new was happening, it was the same routine as always, until the neighbor brings her something new that morning.

— Telephone, girl, and it seems to be urgent!

Answering the phone, she receives the best news of her life and takes a leap of joy. It was Vinicius, confirming his trip with him for the vacation tour he would take with his family. Gradually, everything seemed to be falling into place.

— Hey Dona Maria, I'm going to travel!

— Good, Miss Nathalia, have fun!

Maria adored Nathalia, despite being soft to help her with domestic services. She hoped that one day she and her only son would get along, start dating. I wanted to have her as a daughter-in-law, but it seemed impossible, because the girl dreamed big.

He was looking for boyfriends far away. She returns home bright and arouses her sister's curiosity, always alert to everything that happened to her.

— So, sis, who called you, the rich white guy?

— Himself!

— Sure, to take you to the zoo again

— No, you jealous, this time we are going to travel to a place that he and his family have in the countryside, I will spend my holidays taking a bath in a stream in a good way

Nathalia was happy to realize that she was finally going to have the chance to meet future in-laws, but what she didn't know was that they were unaware of her existence, as her boyfriend never mentioned about their relationship. In the end it would be just one of several playboy friends.

In order not to cause any inconvenience, the boy took the girl to the mall and provided her with new clothes and shoes, all so that her humble origin was not immediately noticed by her parents. The trip took place over a weekend and a huge number of people took a luxurious bus that transported everyone to the Rio dos Vales site, owned by the very rich family.

Many other young people from the Gonsalves Dias school, where Vinicius was studying, were also invited to participate in the tour, all so that the presence of the favela was not seen with great importance.

— I didn't know that all these people were coming with us, I thought you had invited me on this trip in order to be introduced to your parents!

— No, first I will try to bring you closer to my family and, at the most opportune moment, I tell them about our courtship

— I understand, you are afraid that they will not accept me just because I am a poor person, am I not?

— It's not like that, honey, is that these things are complicated, they need to be well elaborated before putting into practice

— I don't see any complications, Vinicius, just arrive with your parents and say that I am your girlfriend!

— You do not understand...

— You have nothing to understand.

If you're not ashamed of me for being poor, give me another explanation for this whole mystery! Wow, I was happy with life, when you invited me to come on this trip, I thought you had already talked about me to your parents and they wanted to know me. When I get here, I meet all the classmates at school and start to be seen as just one of their friends in the crowd!

— You yourself complained that I kept you away from my family, so I had the idea to bring you with me, now do you complain?

— It turns out that I didn't want to be here as your little friend from school, but as your girlfriend!

— But everyone here knows we dated

— Yes, schoolmates, but your family doesn't even dream of that possibility!

When they arrived at the place, they were free to have fun, there was a beautiful stream with crystal clear waters, many fruit trees and a large soccer field. However, throughout the week Vinicius remained strange and avoided being seen by his family next to the girl, who reacted indignantly with the situation.

— Because you stay so far from me, Vinicius. You just want to be with me on the sly, behind the trees or in places where we can't be seen, are you ashamed of me?

— It's nothing like that, baby, your impression

— Print a pineapple! You spend all the time with your little friends and I stay on the sidelines, only come to talk to me when it suits you, we are here for days and you haven't introduced me to your parents yet. What's yours after all, are you going to tell them we're dating or not?

— What bag, girl, stop in such a hurry?

— Well, look here, you fear, if you are a coward to the point of not being able to tell them that we are together, I will!

— You're crazy, girl, don't even think about it!

— Vinicius I'll give you an ultimatum: Either you assume our relationship at once before everyone here or it will be over between us, you decide!

— Holy God, what a terrible girl!

Nathalia ends that conversation, determined to put an end to dating if the boy didn't make a final decision on the case, she wanted to be recognized as part of the important family. Among the boys present there was one who lived staring at the beautiful teenager.

It could be your big chance to hit him against the wall and get him to wake up to make a decision more quickly. She saw in this the possibility of putting pressure on her boyfriend, causing him to be jealous and started to give special attention to the new suitor, who wasted no time and soon approached that beautiful girl, with long hair and greenish eyes.

When he noticed the atmosphere between the two Vinicius, he was jealous and went on to violence against him who flirted with his girl. The two engaged in a fierce exchange of punches and a crowd of onlookers made a circle, while the young men punched each other.

The show lasted only a few minutes and was soon stopped by some of the men who were guarding the place. Because they were important people, they kept the place under strict surveillance. Then the boy's parents wanted explanations of why he was violent, since he had never acted in such a way before.

— Can you start explaining yourself, little boy, what violence was that?

— Really, my son, what happened to act that way with the poor boy? We never saw you angry like that!

— This is a matter that concerns only me and that asshole, please stay out!

— How is it, boy? We are your parents and you owe us explanations!

— Dad, could we talk about it another time? It's just that I'm not in a position to explain them now

— Pay attention, Vinicius, tomorrow, gather all your friends and return as soon as possible to Belem. The tour is over, do we understand?

— Damn it!

The young man withdraws dissatisfied with the decision made by the father, that night he and Nathalia did not speak, a bad atmosphere hung over the couple. The next morning everyone was already on the bus back to the city and they remained without any communication. The silence during the return trip was broken only by the noise of the vehicle's engine and the rippling of the winds that whistled on the side of the windows that were ajar. What should have been a diversion ended in a violent and unpleasant way. But she had a positive point in all of that, now the teenager had awakened in her boyfriend the certainty that if she did not position herself in the face of the relationship, she could lose her. Virginia was one of the few girls at school with whom Nathalia talked.

And exchanged confidences, they traveled side by side and she decided to start a dialogue with her friend to understand the meaning of everything that happened the afternoon of the previous day.

— Can you explain to me what the hell happened yesterday? — Asked another teenager the friend who continued looking out the window, as if she was lost in thought, very distant — Why did you keep flirting with that boy if you knew you would end up confused?

Silence was his only answer, so insist with the question

— Hey, can you answer, please?

— What did you say?

— I asked what happened to you to make Vinicius jealous with that boy, did you see what his inconsequential attitude did?

— Sometimes you speak just like my sister, full of reason!

— Speak softly, you don't need everyone on the bus to hear our conversation

— I can't speak softly like you!

— Well try because it's time to educate yourself, after all, if you want to conquer your space in the society to which your boyfriend belongs, it is essential that you educate yourself

— I got tired of wasting time with this idiot. I thought he was going to take advantage of this trip to introduce me as a girlfriend to his parents, but that was never his intention. If I had known that he would put me in the position of one more of his friends from school, he wouldn't have come!

— I already said that you are pushing too hard…

Wanting to be included in this family by force

— What I can't do is waste time, I need to solve my life right away!

— Talk low, damn it ...

— It will hurt you, okay?

— Wow, but how much stupidity in one person

— If you know I'm like that, stupid, why do you still insist on talking to me?

— I'm your friend and friends are just like that, imbeciles who live trying to help others and getting slapped in the face

— Sorry, come on, I'm really thick!

— Wow, you apologizing to me? It will rain heavily today ...

The two, exchange laughter and the journey continues for another hour, then everyone was on solid ground, returning to their homes. Nathalia decides to go with her friend and spent the rest of that day in her company, then she goes downhill to face her sad slum reality.

As for the boyfriend, he didn't even know what he was going to do after all that miserable confusion, after all, he didn't want to talk to her anymore after what happened. But that's okay, I wouldn't regret the attitude I took.

Because it was necessary to put pressure on the playboy, now I had to wait and see what would result, the young man's parents insisted that he explain himself.

— Vinicius, we need to end our conversation, I and your father need to understand what happened there in the place between you and that boy

— Okay, mom, I'll explain. I realized he was hitting on my girl...

And I couldn't help it, I went for violence

— But what girl is that, my son, since when do you have a girlfriend? Well, at least we know

— Her name is Nathalia I hadn't introduced them yet because there are some details to be exposed before

— And how did you meet her if you almost never leave home? Are you a girl from our church, do you belong to the same social level, are you the daughter of someone we know, or are you part of that group of friends you decided to take on the tour to the farm?

— No, father, she does not belong to our social circle nor is she the daughter of wealthy or important people

— Jesus Christ! My son, we always gave you the best education and guided you with what types of women we wanted you to get involved with.

— Mother, you said that because we are Christians, we should not show respect for people, prejudice does not match our faith

— Do not mix things up, boy, it is not prejudice against this or that person, but we cannot allow our only son and heir to all our wealth to end up falling into the hands of a profiteer

— So that's it, you are not concerned with my feelings but with the money you have? And my happiness, where is it?

— Your father is absolutely right, my son, we did not build all this heritage with so much sacrifice for you now to waste with your love adventures

— Adventures? Mother I love this girl and I intend to marry her

— Don't even think about such madness, boy, it will never happen!

— The usual dictator, isn't he my father? Everyone must accept his impositions without arguing ...

— Think how you want, but I will not allow you to commit this madness. Even if for that I have to send him away from here to another state or even another country!

I did not raise a child to hand over to gunmen like these, you can keep taking that interest out of your head. And final point, there is no more talk about this subject in this house! The young man learned from an early age to respect his parents' decisions, even when they did not match his ideals, so he fell silent and did not carry out his own defense.

He was well aware of his father's imperative stance and understood it was a waste of time trying to change his views on any subject. However, his mother with that special kind of wife always managed to tame him and needed to convince her to accept Nathalia, so there would be hope of getting her included in the family, but meanwhile, in the favela:

— Wow, do you mean the playboy went purple with jealousy and pitched the biggest shack?

— Yeah!

— I could never imagine that with all that speck of fine-grained he would go down the level and set off for violence!

— Because it went down, it proves that we are all the same. Rich or poor, when they lose their time, they do the same crazy things. Will he still come looking for you?

— You know what? Damn it! Bad luck if he doesn't come!

— My daughter, God writes in crooked lines and if by chance your courtship with this guy ends it is because it was the best

— Thank you, mother, because you are not much to support my attitudes

— It was a mistake on your part to want to make the boy jealous, so at the very least you should apologize

— I will not crawl, my sister, let him touch himself and come after me. I told you that if we didn't make our relationship official with his parents, I would end it all!

— Well, each sentence has a sentence. If you think that way, so be it

— It will be that way!

The month of the holidays coincided with the strong summer of the North region and at that time of the year the rains stop almost completely, the climate warms up and the heat becomes almost unbearable. Nathalia and her family went to the beach several times and enjoyed themselves as much as they could. Since the money was always tight, it was barely enough to maintain the house and the spare change that was left over was used to pay for public transport tickets and to eat some cheap snacks that were sold there.

Despite maintaining a firm stance as to the idea that she would not be worried about her boyfriend's permanent absence, deep down the girl was extremely worried and sometimes thought of calling the boy in search of an explanation that would allow her to conclude whether they were going to continue. together or not. However, she remained steadfast in her position as an unyielding woman and true to her purpose of not humiliating herself, as she said she would.

Despite being a slum, it needed to have a minimum of dignity, it would not crawl. The month of July ended and the following week he would return to classes in the hope of being able to see Vinicius at school again, the moment of truth arrived, his destiny would be revealed there.

The first day of August began under heavy rain, the summer ended and the winter routine that usually lasted the eleven months of the year began again. Studying in the morning had its disadvantages in a region where you wake up under heavy storms.

Always go out with your father who went to work early and guaranteed your safety. That Monday the two would meet again after almost thirty days without seeing each other. Arriving at the school the first person with whom she kept in touch was Virginia, always interested in the news.

— Hi, friend, finally back to school

— Back to the sacrifice, yes!

— Always complaining about life ...

— You know very well that I hate to study!

— It turns out that without study there is no guaranteed future for anyone, my friend, we need to be well prepared to face the job market

— It is easier to get rich and not have to work!

— Ah, always dreaming!

— It is not a dream, I will still do well in life and I will show you that with enough money I will have many employees, instead of having to sweat my shirt!

— I know, and how do you intend to get so much money...

Winning in the lottery?

— Damn, silly, I'm going to take off a millionaire wedding!

— Oh really? Well, only if it is with another rich man, because with Vinicius I think it is unlikely after what happened on the tour. Look at him talking to Rafaela, they seem very intimate

— Where?

The two young men talked animatedly, despite the strong splashes of the morning rain that insisted on falling, they were a few meters from where the adolescents passed towards the school.

Everyone else who knew about the relationship between them and what happened on the site commented on the fact that he was talking to someone else and not to his girlfriend. Nathalia blushed, feeling mixed with anger and jealousy.

Confused, she hastened her steps. She entered the classroom as quickly as possible in order to prevent her eyes from continuing to contemplate the scene that inexplicably bothered her, since she never had the slightest passion for her boyfriend. Virginia noticed her distress and wasted no time, asking as usual.

—Wow, friend, what happened to you? I thought I was going to hit the school gate in such a hurry

— Sure, don't you see it's raining?

— Stop talking, woman, we were walking quietly down the street and it was just you seeing Vinicius talking to Rafaela, he almost ran

— You're wrong, I didn't care what I saw! He's the one who knows, if you want to change me for that watery white girl who keeps her, I don't care!

— I know...

The teacher enters the room and the forty students present are silent to hear his teachings. It was the class that the enemy teenager of studies considered more boring. He hated them all, but the ones that involved numbers, calculations and formulas were, in his view, the most abominable.

— Nobody deserves ... Math right in the first class after the holidays?

— Shh! Silence you crazy ...

Vinicius and Nathalia did not remain in the same room in the second half, they were placed in different places. During all the time that the teachers taught the subjects in class, his thoughts were out there, focused on discovering where the boy would be. In a huge school like that, it was the largest in the public school, system. He made plans to go looking for her at recess, counting the minutes for the break.

While the other students struggled to follow the understanding of the subjects in question, she paid little attention to the class and remained staring at the door, as if she hoped that from one moment to the next, he might come up and invite her to talk, do peace. What was happening to her? — Thought while writing the blank page of the notebook. Would have fallen in love with the playboy? No, it was impossible to believe that at the time of the championship was infected with such a mediocre feeling.

She agreed to go out with him just to organize a millionaire wedding, become a woman of many means and leave that small, miserable life there in the slum. Love? Passion? What the hell was that now bothering your heart and shaking your soul every time I imagined he talking to the watery white girl?

— Hey, do you want to stop flying there?

— What's it?

— You are not paying attention in class, did not write anything in the notebook, call me girl. That way you will repeat the year ...

— Ah, I'll get it from your notebook later!

Finally, the break. He barely rang the bell and she hurried out into the school corridor with her uneasy gaze, trying to see the young man somewhere in the wide place. He was looking for him as if he were looking for something very precious, it was the first time that he was interested in seeing him again, not even when they were in good spirits did, he want so much to be able to face him. It only took a few minutes and she found him, but it didn't go the way she expected. Virginia, who stayed close by, tried to comfort her.

— I'm sorry, friend, but I think he's already in another

— Okay...

Vinicius was leaning against the wall next to the school garden, making out with Rafaela, a young proud who was part of the group of rich people and did not relate to the most, humble.

Although the public network at that time included girls and boys from all walks of life, they were like oil over a portion of water, they did not mix.

It seemed that he had chosen to satisfy his parents' opinion and to date a woman of similar social status, breaking up with the beautiful young woman from the favela. At the end of the class she returns home completely unmotivated, despite the words of encouragement from the chatty friend who kept trying to revive her.

— I don't know why you got so low, you told me you didn't love him.

— I never loved anyone, I have no idea what this love or passion might be!

— Then explain why you are so sad?

— I don't know ... Even I'm confused, I never felt that before

— This is love, you played in the playboy my friend

— You are crazy? This never!

— Yes, I did, and I'll tell you something very serious ...

— What?

— You're screwed!

— Don't even tell me ... If that is true, I will be chipped!

— Yes, because he is now in another

— Wants to know? Damn it!

The two lived in the same neighborhood and their houses were located on either street, that is, their backyards were one, separated only by an old wooden fence. After a lunch made with beans, rice and dried fish with açai, the two used to sit under a huge cashew tree, to eat the ripe fruits and vent their frustrations.

— Our names are too big, starting today I call you Nat and you call me Vi, agreed?

— Whatever...

— Credo, woman, cheer you up! Shaking in a low mood, huh?

— Vi, have you ever fallen in love with a boy before?

— You are crazy? I don't waste my time thinking about it, I'm more concerned with my studies

— Just like my sister's annoyance, just think about spending the whole day with your face stuck in books!

— At least soon she will have finished high school, gone to college and got a good job. You, if you don't wake up for life will end in the worst

— Do you know the end of women like you? Graduating in an important profession, marrying a tramp and working to support him and a family of children, I was not born for this kind of stupid situation!

— You are a very insensitive person, dry inside

— Nothing like that, I just see other ways to improve my life without having to spend years staring at books and notebooks. In addition, if one day I will have to walk with a hula hoop on the finger of my left hand and carry a boy in my belly for nine months, all disfigured and destroying my beauty, let it be for a good cause and not for this idiocy of passion!

— Know. And in this case, is the "good cause" you refer to money?

— And what else could it be?

— Mercy!

Second Chapter - The Mansion

Despite being indifferent to her own feelings, Nathalia realized that little by little something was changing inside her, since she lost Vinicius due to the slip she made during the tour. After seeing him with another she felt jealous, she was no longer the same. Jealousy trembled at the base and was bothered by the possibility of never returning to dating again.

The days passed and at school it became more and more difficult to have to live with the criticism of the other young people who laughed at the comic situation she lived in, while her ex-boyfriend was enjoying with another one right under her nose.

Thus, he decided that he would abandon his studies so that he would no longer have to live with that humiliation for a single day. Before making that decision, however, he asked for advice from his best friend who always listened to her and gave him good guidance.

— Dad, we need to talk!

— Is there a problem, young lady?

— Many! Will you buy me a snack?

— Sure, come on your uncle ...

While walking down the street where they lived, towards the snack car, she started to talk to her father about what bothered her and to receive from him the necessary guidance to choose the next step towards the future.

— My daughter, we cannot force you to continue your studies if what you want at that moment is to stop, but I can show you the consequences of your decision: Stop a little and think, what future will you have if you don't finish at least high school and learn a profession so you can have a good job? How will you survive in an increasingly competitive world?

— I totally agree with you, I know you care about me, but Dad, there are other ways to win in life, besides running after work!

— Truth? And what means would these be, entering the world of crime? Becoming a drug dealer or becoming a prostitute? Do you think about using your beauty to make money, becoming a showgirl like many others out there?

— Are you crazy, Dad?" Me, huh!

— Then how else could it be, what do you have in mind? Yes, because the golden egg duck you dated has already fallen out of your life ...

— Yeah, I know that more than anyone else! And that is the main reason for having decided to drop out of school, you can't continue to be snubbed by that fat boy playboy!

- Now things are clearer

- Good night, beautiful uncle!

- Hello, my favorite niece, will you always?

— Yes, with everything I have the right!

While savoring the succulent snack in his father's pleasant company, he vented his pains and sorrows, always receiving support and advice that he considered opportune and indispensable, he was very lucky to be able to count on his friendship, since his mother had no words of encouragement used to hear.

After returning home, he remained awake for most of the night in bed, unable to sleep, being held hostage by a terrible insomnia. But everything seemed to contribute to its own good, as it was possible for him to reflect a little more on everything he heard and learned from Carlos and to make his decisions.

The following week she wasted no more time and closed her school enrollment, would take a break from her studies and pursue her dream of becoming a rich and important woman through other means.

She was a good-looking, tall and attractive young woman, surely there was some other way to achieve her goals. Who did not like to know that she had dropped out of high school was her friend who did not miss the chance to give her a terrible scolding:

— Freaked out, was it crazy? Near the end of the year and are you ready for one of these? Why don't you at least finish your studies and then run after those crazy dreams of yours?

— Sorry, Vi, but I can't stay here at school. It will be unbearable to see this rascal of a fig, mocking me. He makes fun of my face with this watery white girl!

— And since when has it shaken you, woman, whenever a guy like that wanted to humiliate you, he wouldn't immediately put several others in front of them?" After all, what is happening to you, my friend, has softened for this rich man?

— I don't know, it could be! Now I just want to get out of here and fix it far away from that place!

— She is in love and that is very bad, really terrible!

— I will not be regretting, but raise your head and move on! And I'll let you know, if I tell someone I left school because of him, I'll kill you, see?

— Credo, are you crazy?

— Be warned, if you spread this story around, I forget our friendship and break your face!

— Mercy ...

The two friends returned home together, as they were neighbors. Upon arriving at the home, she already found Dona Luiza ready to want further explanations from her daughter about the fact that she had blocked enrollment at the school, since the secretary would have already called the neighbor's phone and reported what had happened. It would get complicated for the teenager, her inconsequence irritated her mother, always agitated and nervous about everything.

— What business is it that I was told on the phone at the school, young lady, that you had her enrollment canceled? Are you crazy for good? Do you have any idea how difficult it was to get a place for you to study at that blessed school?

— I didn't cancel the registration, mom, I just asked them to lock up until next year, then I'll see if I start again!

— And what are you going to do all this time, bum around, roll the bag around corners?

Yes, my daughter, because of two or one, you study to become decent people or become a whore!

— Good God, mother, do you need to talk to her like that?

— I talk to your sister as you see fit, don't get involved where you are not called!

— Poor thing...

— Poor thing is the rat that was born naked, this one does not deserve to be treated like people, he always makes mistakes! Now to finish dropping out of studies in order to be loitering, this girl still kills me with disgust!

For the first time, Nathalia does not respond badly to her mother and listens to the affronts in silence, even her sister found her behavior strange. After being placed under the sewer by the one who was supposed to hear and understand her inner anguish, she climbs the old wooden staircase and is secluded in the cramped room located at the top of the house made of rotten wood, where she slept with her sister

Next week she would be eighteen, it would certainly be the same as always, she would not receive gifts or wishes for happy birthday, she would just be older and without a future.

From the father he would still receive a strong hug and if there were some change left in the wallet they would celebrate in the old style, they would go to the snack car and there he would devour that sandwich on a whim.

Lying on the tanned foam mattress, covered with a sheet extracted from an old hammock, quite thick and prickly on the skin, she looked at the ceiling made of cheap woods and clay tiles.

Stained with mud and decorated with the junk that the insects spread there. I was already used to sharing the space with the cockroaches and spiders that lived there. The sister approaches and tries to give a strength.

— Hi sis, I came here to hear you, in case you need to let off steam ... Mommy took it hard with the words today

— Just today? And since when did Dona Luiza treat me with less ignorance than she did now?

— Give her a discount, my sister, our mother is a bitter and unhappy woman due to the difficult life she always had with our father

— I know that, for this very reason I decided to shut up and not confront it head on as I used to do before, I grew up and understood the reasons for her revolt! And that is why I do not intend to marry a poor man I do not want to one day become a frustrated woman like our mother or to vent my revolt on my children! Well, I don't think that's fair, after all, what is my fault if she wavered and didn't know how to choose the right person to marry?

— You are absolutely right, sis, now I begin to understand your reasons for living trying to get along in life, you don't want to make the same mistake that she did

— Yes, and I advise you to do the same, because this talk of uniting our lives to someone for love is pure idiocy, that idiotic feeling may even bring the illusion of happiness for a while, but then, when children and fantasy are born ends up giving way to reality, what remains is what we see in our parents. The inheritance of what they planted in their failed lives was just total frustration!

— Wow, today you are inspired, talking pretty

— You always saw me as a dumb tomboy, without any wisdom. Empty-headed, isn't it? Well, know that I let myself pass by the donkey of the house and allowed you to occupy the place of genius all the time, snub me and gloat over me. But I talk a lot with our father, who is not a doctor of this or that, in fact poor guy never even finished his primary studies, but he has a knowledge of life that you can't even imagine!

— Oh really? Our father?

— Yes, and listening to your advice I learned more from life than you know by reading these heaps of books!

— Gosh, Nathalia, good to know that I've been cheating with you all this time. But what do you intend to do now that you have abandoned your studies? Are you going to work in a family home or somewhere else?

— Do you know that you just gave me a great idea?

— As well?

— Remember that Dad said that his boss's wife was without a nanny for his little son and asked him to find a girl here in the neighborhood? Has she found someone yet?

— I don't know, just asking

— That's what I will do as soon as he gets home!

Suddenly the two girls start to hear a serious dispute at the bottom of the house, their parents argued vehemently about the question of the daughter leaving school, while Luiza accused the girl of being disinterested, Carlos defended her.

— Nobody is obliged to do what they don't like, woman…

For example I was not born with an open mind for this study business and I didn't die of hunger for that reason. I learned several trades and I never get unemployed

— Ah, but of course, your daughter really took after you! An illiterate father and mother, number one enemy of sitting on a school bench!

— You're right, I didn't really study and I'm the son of a humble couple who didn't study either, but I have much more good manners than you who studied so much

— Do you want to know why I studied and did nothing in life? For the simple reason that I met you and let me be deceived by your appearance as a heartthrob, that's why I screwed myself and today I'm here in this filthy pigsty!

— You have no right to place the blame for your failure on my shoulders, several times I warned you that I was not the right man to enter your life, I am not to blame if you did everything to become my wife

— Anyone who sees you saying these things may even think that I tied a rope around your neck!

— But it was like it was

— Limp, man, did I force you to marry me?

— Yes, she got pregnant on purpose just to arrest me

— My dear, I didn't force you to go to bed with me and if I got pregnant it was because we didn't take the necessary care to avoid the worst!

— Stop talking, woman, you know very well what you did

— Oh yes? And what did I do? Explain me?

— You got pregnant on purpose just to trap me in this filthy, disgusting and unhappy relationship! That's what you did! I knew I never loved you, so you played dirty!

They argued and did not even notice the presence of the two daughters there in the narrow room and the son who had just arrived from work. The most shaken of all with those revelations was Nathalia, who was the oldest and felt the pivot of her parents' unhappiness. Paralyzed, she couldn't get out of the place, run, hide.

They finally realized the situation and the terrible mistake they made in revealing their worst secrets to their children in ways they had never done before. But it was too late, now how to explain to the daughter he loved most that despite everything he did not see her as the culprit for the destruction of her happiness.

It is painful for anyone to imagine that at birth it caused someone's unhappiness and, especially, if they were their parents. Nathalia realized that her mother despised her, but did not understand the real reasons. However, from that moment on everything became clear, she was a child generated without the slightest planning, used as a device by a badly intentioned woman in order to arrest a man who did not love her.

His head became a knot and everything around him seems to have collapsed, it was like suddenly things in his life started to go wrong in sequence, one after the other. Sitting on the curb at the corner of the street in Morava, she is surprised by the arrival of her best friend, who went to explain herself and apologize.

— I'm sorry, daughter, it was not my intention to give you the misconception that your arrival in our lives was a mistake

— But that's exactly what I heard you say to mom!

— Yes, honey, I know, and that's why I came here to explain myself. Really, her mother used her pregnancy in bad faith to force me to marry her. For I knew that even though I am poor, I am a just man of character, I would never abandon a daughter. However, after you were born you made me a very happy man and even today it is the biggest reason for me to live in this world of so much suffering. Things are not easy for us, as you have seen, but having it makes up for all my day-to-day efforts.

— Wow, Dad, speaking like that you even move me!

— So, forgive my harsh words and we will return home, it is not safe to stay here at this time of night

Father and daughter hug and return home, where they had already ended the screams and scandals of hours ago. On the same occasion, Nathalia takes advantage and talks to Carlos about the possibility of working as a nanny for her bosses.

— Father, did your mistress ever find the person she was looking for to take care of her young son?

— I do not know why?

— I want to work, earn my own money and be independent!

— The ideal would be to finish your studies and learn a good profession

— The important thing is to earn money honestly, my father, no matter the job!

— That's right. If you want to work, I'll talk to the boss and see what I can

The Mendes mansion was the largest in the city, located on the main avenue…

And on the corner with the Museum, it occupied a wide area of privileged commercial location. That morning, when the mistress practiced her routine Yoga in the garden, next to the pool, Carlos takes advantage and asks her some questions related to the possible chance of a job for her daughter.

— Good morning, missus, please forgive me for the inconvenience

— Yeah, what is it about?

— It's just that a few days ago you asked me if I wouldn't meet a girl interested in babysitting your son

— Yes, in fact I asked you this question, but it is for companions

— Is that I now have a girl who is available to the service, in case you still need

— Well, we have a lady in the job at the moment, but we still don't know for sure if it will work, because in these cases the ideal would be a younger person. My son, Mr. Carlos, is a child who needs special care. He is autistic and his companion must be patient, docile and willing to follow his daily routine, which is not very easy.

— I understand, I believe that the candidate I intend to introduce you to fits this profile

— Well, let's do it like this: As soon as the thirty days of experience with the lady who is working on this job with our son is over, I will fire her and put this young woman to the test

— Okay, ma'am, let me know the right time to be able to bring you

— Very well

Although not yet a definitive confirmation, it was almost right…

That she would have the chance to apply for his first job, he excited the girl who immediately started making plans on how she would use the salary she would receive for the job. However, his father warned him of the need to comply with the boss's demands-

— My daughter, pay close attention: to remain in the position you will receive at the employer's residence, you must be able to perform the function correctly

— I know it!

— I worry, because one of the things she highlighted is that the boy is special

— Special, how?

— Autistic

— What's that?

— I don't understand much of the subject, but it seems to be a little crazy

— Good God, people, how much lack of information. Autism is a psychiatric illness that causes children to have difficulty communicating, is not very sociable and feels bad in environments with many people. It requires special care, companionship and a lot of patience, who takes care of autistic people cannot scream speak too much self or use the voice with a tone of extreme authority has to be docile with the child

— So, I'm chipped, because as everyone knows, I only talk screaming!

— Yes, my daughter, that's why I said I was worried if you would be the most ideal person to take care of this boy

— My sister, if you really want this job, you will have to work hard to change your rude way of being

— And how am I going to do that in such a short time, Chris, am I a shame to change things?

— Take it easy, I can help you. When are you going to start taking care of him?

— Dad said it could be a month from now, more or less!

— Yes, that's what the boss said

— Great, that's enough. So, let's start training right now

— Now?

— That's right, and to start with, try to lower the tone of your voice as much as possible ...

From that night on, Christina started to educate Nathalia voice, helping her with the correct intonation, teaching the ways to express herself in all ways, both in speaking and in posture. The month passed quickly and it was time to show up for work for an interview with her future employer.

The interview took place in the mansion's spacious living room and the poor girl who was raised far from great refinements could fail to show her admiration for such luxury, her eyes sparkled as she contemplated the chandeliers attached to the high ceiling, the very expensive furniture, the tip and even the floor of the place.

It was all made of black porcelain that matched the pearl yellow color of the walls. Carlos, silently observed all the charm in the gleaming look of the teenager who seemed to be in another world, previously existing only in her dreams of Cinderella. She always wished one day to become a very rich woman, to live the rest of her days in complete luxury and comfort, something worthy of fairy tales, but despite having the beauty of a beautiful princess.

And even having the name of a star in television soap operas, she was born in the most complete poverty and only in her adolescent ambition was she able to imagine such greatness.

— I see that you were enchanted with our house

— There is? Sorry, ma'am, I was just watching. Your house is really beautiful

— No need to apologize, I am aware of the beauty of this place, because I decorated it myself

— Mrs. Bárbara is a decorator of fine environments like this, my daughter

— Really...?

— Actually, I have exercised this craft in the past, today I am the owner of the five largest architecture and interior design companies in the State. But I see that you are the young lady that Mr. Carlos was to bring to the interview, he just didn't know it was his daughter

— Yes, sorry to have omitted this detail, it was pure carelessness on my part

— Okay, it doesn't matter. It is even more comfortable that it be, because you have worked with us for many years and we trust you. But what is your name again, my dear?

— Nathalia, lady. Nathalia do Valle

— But what a beautiful name, was it the father or mother who had that good taste?

— Her mother, missus, but I approved because I thought he was magnificent

— Very well, then she is already delivered in good hands...

You can go back to your duties I will take this girl to my office, where we will have a more formal conversation

— Okay, ma'am, excuse me

— All

— Thank you

From that moment on, the two started the long-awaited interview. Bárbara Mendes was a woman who held a prominent position in the society of Pará, her reputation as an architect, designer and businesswoman, used to overlap others in the field and not even her husband, Edgar Mendes, a renowned engineer and with such prestige had greater admiration on the part of elite.

Talking to a person of such social importance, looking into his eyes and giving precise answers was not easy, but the girl from the favela faced that test without fear and did not fail for a second. This led the millionaire to admire her, accepting her as the new caregiver for her special son and on the same day started her services.

To her delight, João Pedro, the autistic person, immediately became attached to her and they spent all their time playing, interacting admirably. It seemed that the boy's chronic sadness was gone with his arrival. They played ball, swam in the children's pool, used the swings placed near the large garden, watched TV and ate popcorn.

The businesswoman was amazed at the evolution of her son's socialization and thanked God for the new employee. At nightfall father and daughter returned together from work for the first time and when she gets home, she makes a point of exposing everything she saw and lived in that place of her dreams.

Christina placed herself as a listener and did not miss the chance to correct her sister's expression errors, with the intention of keeping her qualified to remain in her first job.

— My sister I never imagined being able to work in a place as wonderful as that one day, it is like in fairy tales, full of luxury and charm everywhere. Everything there is spectacular: the furniture scattered around the house the floor made of large black tiles ...

— Porcelain, daughter, the correct name is porcelain

— Ah, yes, it is. And on the ceiling a huge thing, full of several lamps

— It's called chandelier, you silly

— Have you seen it?

— Only in books and magazines, so it is important to read

— Because I saw it live, sis, they are beautiful!

— Look at the tone of the voice, Nathalia, beware of the intonation

— Okay, but let me finish talking to you: Girl, the house is so big, but so huge that I almost got lost there

— Did you walk around the house instead of the child's caregiver, you crazy?

— Of course not, woman, I was with the crazy guy all the time

— My daughter, don't talk about the child that way, respect his disability

— Okay, dad, sorry. Look, Pedro and I played ball and even took a bath in the pool, everything was wonderful. I can't wait to return tomorrow.

— Congratulations, sis, I wish you luck

— Thanks

— Try to be strong and don't do anything stupid

Nathalia remained firm in exercising her activity as a caregiver for the boy Pedro, spent the whole day at the Mendes' mansion and only returned in the late afternoon, always in the company of her father. Gradually she managed to convince him to interact with other children on weekends or holidays.

Accompanying him through the city parks, but always with his mother and father. Although the two entrepreneurs had little free time, they agreed to contribute to the therapy. Pedro was ten years old, but he had the mental characteristics of a much younger child, as he spent most of his time indoors.

And only left when taken to the doctor or school for autistic people, a place he hated. With the arrival of the young woman he was more comfortable and let go of the psychological bonds that previously afflicted him.

Going on walks in the company of the teenager did her so well that her mother asked the girl to live permanently in the mansion, which made her jump with joy. But in order for this to be possible, full authorization from his parents was necessary, as he was still a minor, and that weekend the whole family gathered in the small room to make this decision at the request of Carlos.

— And that's it, guys, the boss wants Nathalia to move to her job permanently and I decided to bring everyone together here to resolve this issue, I would like to hear the opinion of each one of you on this

— I give full support, I believe she has matured a lot during the time she started working and I believe it is something positive for her life, she even learned to communicate better

— Yes, thanks to you my sister

— It also depended a lot on your efforts, sis

— I stay with Chris, if it's working it should go on, when I started working in the workshop, I felt more useful at home

— Thanks bro

— What about you, as a mother, what do you have to say?

There was a brief wordless space in the room before an answer was heard, then the silence was broken:

— I have nothing against this girl working is better than hanging around wandering around with these idle, molasses in this slum. But it is good to take this opportunity seriously, you tomboy, see if you are not going to get ready there and put everything to waste. Do not cause problems in someone else's home to avoid harming your father, as he has worked there for many years and is a trusted employee of the bosses, do not embarrass him

— Do not worry, although you always see me as a problem, I guarantee that I will not be responsible for Dad's dismissal from the job

— Hey, shall we control the mood? We don't gather here for that!

— Didn't they ask for my opinion? So, that's what I had to say on the subject. Talk to your daughter, Carlos, be careful not to complicate your life with your bosses, because where she puts her feet only causes damage!

After these words Luiza withdraws and leaves behind a disappointing silence that blew the eldest daughter's heart, seemed to take pleasure in causing her incurable wounds and did it again with such criticism.

And through such harsh words:

— Calm down, my sister, don't mind our mother's bitterness

— That's it, raise your head and move on sis

— Well, now that my princess is employed and will be full of money in a few days, it's time to repay and pay snacks for all of us!

— That's right!

— Opportunists!

The young woman spent a last weekend at home, with her family and on Monday she left with her belongings for the Mendes mansion, starting a new chapter in her history there. However, it would actually be the worst part of his sad existence.

Until then, the new employee of the mansion imagined that the Mendes were limited to the existence of only three members, their bosses and little Pedro. But, to his surprise, after six months a young couple arrived at the mansion and were announced as the oldest children of Barbara and Edgar, their bosses.

As Nathalia had free access to all rooms of the house, it was easy to meet her daily with the newly arrived boy and in the first contact of the two her eyes met in a special way, causing a strange sensation inside that beautiful girl of blue eyes and long hair, able to bewitch any heart. Leaving her groundless, lost in her feelings.

Third Chapter - The Loss of Innocence

It was the first time that something had confused her that way, she did not understand what had really happened, she was paralyzed in front of the boy, frozen, unable to continue her walk through the corridor of the spacious mansion.

For a few seconds she felt suspended from the floor and intense heat rose from her feet to her head. Only with much effort did she manage to get out of there feeling completely invaded by that look. Luciano was a man of twenty-five years, tall.

Athletic body and a physical posture that can sigh any woman's breath. His honey-colored eyes and a well-detailed beard on his face enchanted the young woman who for the first time found herself dominated by masculine charm and finally discovered the dominating power of passion.

What the innocent girl did not know was that first love always disappoints more than any other and carries the mark of pain, deception and illusion on the packaging. That gleam in the eyes of the young millionaire could even represent the realization of a dream for an almost naive girl, who had just left poverty to live the fantasy of a Cinderella.

But deep down it was just a deep chasm where she would certainly fall and descend until she hit her head on the tip full of stones and thorns, causing the most intense emotional wound in her being.

The girl who was barely eighteen returned to work still confused in her feelings, seeing that the prince charming in the hallway of the mansion amazed her, when she went to live there, she did not imagine that her lover had an adult son and, therefore, beautiful.

See how things are going — she thought, while taking care of Pedro in another room in the house — before always trying to run over a rich man she met at school, she planned to force a pregnancy and secure a millionaire marriage. And now she thanked God for not working, especially after hearing her parents' outburst.

 In addition to discovering that her mother acted the same way and ended up frustrated for the rest of her life. Now fate placed her in the middle of a family that was much more powerful economically and in front of a charming boy.

But the memory of the words of the mother who advised him not to step on the ball, in order not to embarrass the father's name in front of the bosses, kept echoing in his mind.

He was unable to hesitate and give reasons for Senhora Luiza to step on her head, put her failure on Carlos face and ironically say: I didn't warn you! None of this, she would know how to behave with dignity. Did she really know?

— Hi, how are things going here, any news?

— Doctor Luciano, what a pleasure to have you back at this house, is more mature, more beautiful

— Come on, you don't need that much formality with me, you've been living here since I was born and you know I was always the most beautiful man in the world

— Yes, I know, the usual one!

— But, explain to me, who is that beauty that I came across in the hall just now?

— Who, the daughter of Carlos?

— And who is that?

— The porter, boy!

— Ah, I know, I remember him. It's a beautiful tomboy

— Look, don't make fun of the girl, she is even smaller!

— Oh really? That size? I thought I had more than twenty

— And there is something else, the girl comes from a poor family, from the slum. It is certainly not your level and neither the boss will approve the involvement of the two of you

— Calm down, I didn't say I'm going to date the girl

— I know very well what kind of cheap conqueror you have become, you darn, I know your fame up close!

— Definitely the women in this house do not see me with good eyes

— Maybe because my little brother is the naughty type!

— Mrs. Sandra, do you want me to have something prepared for you?

— Stop with this lady, I'm only twenty-three years old

— Now that we spent some years in France, she sees us as if we were her bosses

— Now, and they happen to be?

— You are in this house since I got along, I see you more as a grandmother than as a maid

— Look, you'll end up accustoming me badly, when I start to play grandma don't complain!

— But you were always a boring old woman with all of us, worse than our grandmothers

— Well, keep an eye on that hired brother of yours, see?

— Oh yeah, and why?

— You're getting mad at a girl who works here at the mansion, she just bumped into her in one of the halls of the house

— But what a craze you have to go on hitting on every woman that crosses your path, my brother! And who is this girl?

— She was hired by the boss to take care of your little brother

— Pedro? There, I saw her when I went to see him, that girl was really beautiful. But don't worry, I'll keep an eye on this cheap conqueror

— You don't really change did you have to report me to that jealous little sister?

— That's why I said, so she keeps an eye on you, you kid!

— But look, it even changed the way of treating me, where did Dr Luciano end up?

— The cat ate, didn't he ask me to stop formality? Now let's get out of the kitchen, let the employees work. Come on! Come on!

Joana was the oldest employee in the house and became a type of housekeeper. Mendes' children lived abroad for many years, attending college in France, Patricia graduated in Medicine and Luciano in Law, despite her young age.

In the weeks that followed Luciano and Nathalia meetings around the mansion's wide space were almost constant and, when that didn't happen naturally, they always managed to provide a way to see each other. Joana and Patricia were watching and seeing the danger that the young woman ran in becoming another statistic in the huge list of women victims of the gallantry of Brother Conqueror, decided to warn her to avoid an end where she would regret the folly.

— Hi, we've introduced ourselves, I'm your boss's daughter

— Yes, Dona Patricia, I remember

— It doesn't need so much formality, we are equally young, call me Patricia

— Okay, I'm sorry

— Nathalia, isn't it?

— Yes

— I came to you because we need to have a very serious conversation

— Did I do something wrong?

— Not yet, I hope ... But from what I've realized, you risk doing it and I'm here to try to stop it

— Okay, then explain to me what this is about

— It's about your visible interest in my brother. This is extremely dangerous for your happiness, girl

— Sorry, but I'm not interested in ...

— Do not play the game, girl, you know what I'm talking about. Not only me, but other employees of the house have already realized that the two of you have been meeting on purpose in the corridors and that you no longer stay at your place of work any longer. He has been leaving my brother Pedro alone in his room to move around the other rooms hoping to find Luciano, even hearing rumors that they are making out.

— No, believe me, it hasn't happened yet!

— Still? This means that it is about to happen, right? Look here young lady, pay close attention to what I am going to tell you: Luciano is my older brother, but he does not have a minimum of judgment in that head.

It is unpredictable, adventurous and quite irresponsible, especially when dealing with women. There is a huge row of them crying out their virginities thrown away and you will be next on his list if you don't get out of the abyss as soon as possible

— Don't worry, Patricia, I'll avoid

— Understand one thing: I am not telling you these things in order to discriminate against you.

Claiming that you do not have the same social level as him, but to avoid seeing another girl being used and then discarded by a man who seems give no value to women. Also, think of all the harm this will cause you, such as your expulsion by my mother from that house, your father's resignation and the shame you will bring to your family. Without considering the risk of an unwanted pregnancy

— No, God forbid, that would be terrible!

— So, make sense and set your feet on the ground, no crazy adventures, girl!

— Okay, thanks for the advice

— It was not advice, Nathalia, but warnings

The sermon heard from Patricia was as if it were a slap in the face of Nathalia who trembled at the base, she seemed to be listening to her mother playing in her face that she only served to make trouble wherever she went, she felt her cold blood in her veins and for a second he saw the world collapse on his hard head.

Things were going very well and it would not be prudent on your part to put everything to waste. His father, Carlos, risked the good reputation he had for years with that family just to get him a job opportunity, he could not disappoint him.

He remembered his mother's harsh words when warning him of the risk that it would be to put her there, how could he allow her to be right? However, would it be right to give up that rich opportunity? After all, who could guarantee that Patricia was telling the truth about her brother? What if I was just interested in making her give up on him for being poor? What if he was indeed a scoundrel? Or, if on the contrary, in the end it had character? There were so many doubts, so many questions going through your confused mind ...

The truth would appear right before your eyes at the right time, but at that moment you would have to live with all those uncertainties, because everything in life happens at its right time. The routine followed its normal course, took care of little Pedro and peace still reigned around. Patricia and Joana kept watching the two young people, however, the teenager started to avoid the usual encounters with the seductive Luciano through the halls of the mansion. Well, at least for a while.

— It seems that the girl has lowered the fire and has been dodging Luciano

— I had a serious conversation with her, days ago

— Was it? So, the girl's sudden behavior change is explained. But Patricia, you don't waste any time, do you?

— Knowing my brother as I do, Joana, I could not just cross my arms and see another maid being abused by that adventurer

— You did the right thing, my daughter, I hope she follows your advice., do it to the letter and avoid the worst

— I explained the situation well, if you insist you will break your face as it has happened with the others who passed by this house before and the bad luck will be all hers

— Yes, because his parents will not allow him to marry a girl of her level, a slum

— Not even far, Joana, the damage will be only that poor girl

The two women talked while watching Pedro and his assistant playing in one of the many toys displayed in the mansion's courtyard.

There was a huge contrast between the expression of joy in the little autistic and the apparent sadness on Nathalia face.

— Mom is right, Pedro very happy in the company of this girl

— Yeah, we can't deny it, so it will be a great loss if the worst happens

— It won't happen, Joana, I won't allow it

— I do not know...

The maid doubted the young woman's ability to escape the bad influence of the conqueror because she knew him very well, she had never before known a single of her victims to resist his charm. Rich, good looking and terribly seductive.

A plate full to the ambitious eyes of the poor girls of the city or naive of the countryside, who feed the bad idea that a man like that will give them the due value and put a ring on his left hand, take them to the altar and share with them part of your assets.

In fact, the reality is different, famous marry famous and rich with millionaires. Everything is a matter of pure financial interest, the power of money is the loudest in their world, passion and love are far from their ideals. Despite choosing to live in the mansion, in order to be able to be more present with the autistic boy, Nathalia was entitled to a free day every month.

To return to the parents' house, visit the family. That particular Sunday she left the mansion, when, when passing through the entrance, she realized that Luciano's car, who proposed to give her a ride, stopped beside her. At first, she refused, but due to the boy's enormous insistence he gave in and agreed that he should take her home. After he started working, he joined forces with his father and brother, building a new home, with more space and comfort.

It was possible to give a room for each of them and buy new furniture. A stove and a brand, new refrigerator for your mother, in addition to other advantages. So, he had no ceremony to take the new playboy there, which made the neighborhood's eyes widen and gossip, as they immediately imagined he was her new boyfriend or lover.

Throughout the journey from the city center to the poor neighborhood located on the outskirts, Luciano tried in every way to convince the girl to allow him more space in his life, however, remembering Patricia guidelines she avoided as much as she could. Finally, they arrived at the destination and after thanking the ride and avoiding a forced kiss, he left the luxurious car and went to his parents' house under the strong eyes of the envious.

— Hi my sister, I was waiting for you, tell me the news!

— There are many, a full bucket! Hi dad, hi mom...

— Is there no more "father blessing" and "mother blessing"? This youth of today ...

— Blessing grandpa, how are you, all in peace?

— Um, God give you judgment, you crazy!

— Ah, ah, ah, always in a bad mood! And my grandmother, how are you?

— It goes well, I didn't want to come, it stayed there with the chickens and the pigs. He asked when her favorite granddaughter will have the cadence to visit her, I said it will only be after she is dead and buried

— Any weekend like that, I'm going to visit her, it won't be long

— Come, Patricia, I want to know everything ...

The two sisters go up to the upper floor of the new house, which is wider and more comfortable. Christina continued her studies and was already in the first year of medical school, got a scholarship and studied at the largest and most important State University. She got her own room after the construction, and she was always grateful for all the help she received, as well as being curious about the older sister's unknown current life.

— Wow, your room looks like a stuffed animal store

— Ah, look who's talking, did you happen to send this bunch of animals?

— They were from Pedro, son of the boss, he didn't want more and they were going to be thrown away, so I asked. Imagine, all this being thrown in the trash, what a waste!

— No doubt. But come on, woman, tell me the news!

— Wow, my sister, I won't even tell you. When I went to live in the mansion, I did not imagine that my bosses had other children besides Pedro

— Dammit, is there?

— Yes, a couple who were studying abroad in Paris

— Caracas, these Mendes are important people, right? It's my big dream to know France, to walk around the Eiffel Tower ...

— Hey, hello, go back to earth, woman!

— Let me dream a little!

— You are an intelligent, studious woman, you are already graduating as a doctor. In a few years you will get along and be able to go wherever you want, to see the whole world

— God hear you ... But, continue where I interrupted you

— It turns out that now they have returned here and are in the mansion

— They who?

— Oh, Chris, tune you woman! The mistress's children!

— Yes, So, sis, what does that worry you about?

— Well, it turns out that the boy is a charm, a real prince!

— Nathalia do Valle, you have your mind! Remember everything our mother said on the day Dad decided to put you inside that house, he won't let her have a chance to step on him

— I know, I thought of all that, but he hasn't left me alone since the first day we met

— Is your mistress's son hitting on you?

— Girl, when we ran into one of the mansion's corridors I almost died of fright!

— But didn't you say that the boy is the biggest presence?

— Oh, what a donkey you got, huh? Where's my great little sister, disappeared?

— Sorry, but my intelligence is in another area

— The unfortunate is darn beautiful, that's the big problem, it's hard to resist his charm! Today when he left the mansion, he offered to bring me here and he was so insistent that he couldn't refuse, I ended up accepting

— Did anything happen between you while you came here?

— No, he tried to kiss me, but I refused

— Good God, my sister, I already saw that things will not end well for you

— I don't know what to do, every time I approach him, I lose my head and just think about throwing myself in his arms

— Can't you see that this is a huge bore? When will a thin man, a millionaire and have the woman he wants in life take his relationship with a poor girl like you seriously? You lost track of things, did you? He will only use you and then throw it away

— You're talking just like Patricia

— And who is that?

— His sister came to me a few days ago to warn that his brother is a bad character, who has a habit of abusing maids and then leaving

— Good heavens, the sister herself has already stated that the individual sucks!

— Yes, sis, but what if she is only trying to get away from him because I am poor?

— It touches you, my sister, if that were the reason it was enough to have revealed what was happening to the parents and they would send you away once and for all

— You think?...

— Of course, girl, in my opinion she only tried to help you by knowing the attitudes of her bad character

— Oh, Chris, I'm lost and not knowing what to do

— It's always like that, the poor little girl dreaming of being a Cinderella. Wake up my sister, fairy tales don't exist in the real world!

— I'll confess something to you, sis, I think for the first time I'm really in love

— Jesus, Mary and Joseph. Now screw it!

— I totally chipped!

The conversation continued for several hours, Christina tried to convince her sister to give up trying to live that dangerous love story and to guard against a possible disappointment. On the other hand, Nathalia said she had no strength to renounce her feelings for Luciano, she felt completely overwhelmed by passion that invaded her heart from the first moment that her gaze merged with his.

After opening up with Chris, he talked to his friend Virginia, the confidant who was his neighbor, and received from her the same advice that he should really run away from such a precipice. However, the advice he received seemed to be unable to find a place in his confused and ambitious mind because of the unlikely possibility of doing well in life.

The truth is that the teenager still had the desire to marry a millionaire and become an important person in society, she knew that this was possible due to the immense beauty she possessed. But, what he did not realize was that this purpose could throw him at the bottom of the well. On Monday she returns to the workplace, where the daily routine resumes. That night, she was already in her rooms, when she was past twenty-two o'clock, she heard footsteps in the narrow corridor that led to her room located in an isolated part of the other rooms of the mansion. Believing it was Joana, who used to pass by to check that all the employees who slept there were properly accommodated.

She opens the door to ask the housekeeper for permission to go to the kitchen in search of something to eat, as she inexplicably felt very hungry, despite to have dined. However, it was not the elderly woman, but an unexpected figure who intended to find her there, in order to get closer. As soon as she became visible at the entrance to her room, she was pushed back inside by two strong hands, it was Luciano who used the opportunity to steal a moment of caresses or something much more serious than that.

The girl was pushed back inside her rooms and leaning against one of the walls, there she was suffocated by an unexpected kiss and when she felt the curl of that light beard with a mustache on her lips and the smell of the French perfume that exhaled in her nostrils, he immediately identified it as the charming young man who boldly decided to invade the place to steal his charms as a woman.

Lost between the fright of the invasion and the pleasure of being kissed by that prince charming, she was not sure if she screamed or gave herself up completely. Doubt was dominated and for the first time was kissed madly

He tried to throw her on the bed, she resisted as long as she could, he persisted relentlessly and no longer had the strength to refuse what his body also wanted, burning inside with the flames of desire that consumed her uncontrollably, ended up allowing her to lie on the bed. that bed's soft mattress while she was undressed.

Those huge, yet soft hands caressed her body, shivering from the intensity of the pleasure she felt with each touch, her fingers slid over his warm, virgin skin, still untouched and possessed. The boy was experienced, he knew how to drive a woman crazy by the loving touch and at the same time manly, strong, electrifying! In a few minutes she was totally naked on the bed, without the nightgown and underwear she was wearing before.

It became an easy prey, tied by the heart to an almost unknown lover who arrived in his life to stay. She was lost, there was no longer any connection in her mind with prudence or reality, she fell down the precipice, into the vague illusion of first love. Not even the fact that the door to the room had been unlocked prevented her from surrendering, she was not worried about the worst, the words of her mother who long ago warned of that danger resonated for a few seconds in her subconscious, her voice seemed to be real, but the whisper of that hot mouth at the base of her ears was stronger, more intense, much more powerful and controlled her.

— Stop, please!

— I will not stop I know you want ...

— Good God, help me ...

— I am your god, your desire, your passion ...

—Then own me right away, at once ...

Gradually his purity is undone, his intimacy feels invaded, he acts delicately, but with all the strength he needs to fully enter his bowels and allow passage for incomparable pleasure.

That first experience lasted only a few hours, but it seemed like an eternity, now it was entirely his. But did he also belong to you? That answer would only give time to the naive girl who made the terrible mistake of believing that it was possible to live a beautiful love story with an adventurer, unable to love and care for the feelings of those with whom she just had fun, without any other pretensions. Those meetings continued to take place for some time in the wee hours of the night, always at the risk of being seen by someone.

Especially by Joana, who used to move around the mansion keeping an eye on other employees. The housekeeper suffered from insomnia and spent part of the night wandering the halls. The irresponsibility of the young philanderer was so great that he was not even careful to use a condom at the time of sexual intercourse in order to avoid a possible pregnancy.

And she, without any experience in the matter, gave herself to him several times without worrying about this detail, because she was sure that in case this were to happen, they would get married, since surely the boy would not leave a child in the abandonment. And, in her stupid way of thinking, even if that were to happen her parents would not abandon her with a grandson in the womb, as he would be a Mendes and that name was extremely valuable, there could not be a seed of them thrown in the gutter. It can be seen that even though she was truly in love, she still carried in her heart that old flame of ambition that led her several times to want to hit the belly of the rich boyfriends she was lucky enough to conquer with her beauty.

And that would be the cause of his misfortune, because Luciano Mendes was a bad character who would not be moved by the fact that he knew that there was a child inside his womb and neither would his parents admit such a union. They would not allow the heir of all his assets to join a slum with no future like that. Patricia, her sister-in-law, tried to warn her of the danger she was in, but she was ambitious and didn't want to hear it.

Now the mistake had already been made, it was time to reap the negative results of their attitudes. The end of that month came and Christmas was approaching, it had been days since the teenager had been weakened, without mood, with the fallen appearance, pale and with retching of vomit. However, he did not complain to the bosses about anything.

Luciano disappeared from the mansion more than two weeks ago, but she dared not interrogate anyone to find out about him, avoiding showing any particular interest to him, as this would raise serious suspicions.

However, he was shocked when he heard Patricia commenting with Joana on her brother's sudden disappearance, making a trip almost hastily back to Paris. Staying hidden in some corner of the kitchen.

In order not to be seen by the two women and at the same time listen to the conversation, she felt suspended from the floor with the statements of the supposed sister-in-law.

— You know, Joana, I'm worried

— Is there? And with what?

— As I told you, the fact that Luciano invented this sudden return to Paris is very suspicious

— And when that mischievous kid doesn't act suspiciously in everything he does?

— Joana, wake up, things can be more serious than we think

— Geez, so you worry me! Do you think he was getting into trouble around there?

— No, as we well know the only confusion, he could have been involved in would be with women

— Truth

— And that's where the problem lies. What has my irresponsible little brother been up to?

The two, stare at each other while Patricia takes a cup of hot coffee that the old housekeeper had just served her:

— Jesus Christ, girl, I don't even want to imagine such a thing!

— Well, I've been thinking about this possibility for a long time. What if that unfortunate Nathalia gave in to his charms and gave himself up on an adventure that will end up destroying her life completely?

— My God, I hope we are only considering such a possibility, my daughter

— I don't know, Joana, have you noticed how pale she is, disfigured and without that disposition from before? It looks like you're pregnant!

— Oh, my Lady, don't even tell me such a disgrace! Poor girl, if this really happened, she is lost

— But if so she herself will be the only one to blame, because it was not for lack of warnings

— I know that, Patricia, but as women we know what we are capable of doing for love, we commit many follies!

— Sorry, Joana, but I can't agree with this idea that every woman one day goes crazy with passion. You know me very well, since I was a child, and you know I was never given to liking boys the same age as me.

I always found them very irresponsible and tried to relate to the elders. I had my first sexual experience at the age of seventeen in Paris and with a man who was three times my age, but I practiced the conscious act that was what I wanted and the right time. I never lost my mind for anyone

— Yes, my daughter, but not all of us are the same.

I myself was one of those who lost his head and went on an adventure that cost me happiness for the rest of my life

— You, Joana? Well, who knew, I thought I never even slept with a man

— Hey, I wasn't born old like that tomboy, I was also a child, teenager and lived my youth intensely. At least until I met that fret that destroyed my peace

— Let's take an hour for you to tell me more about your story, it seemed interesting. Now let me go to the clinic, I need to work

The listener, who remained hidden until that moment listening to the conversation, leaves towards her rooms and sits there on the bed where for several nights she made love to her seducer, desperate to realize the madness she had committed. Luciano went back abroad without even saying goodbye, used and abused her, then he left as Patricia warned she would do.

And now, what to do? What would be her destiny, when everything was revealed, how Dona Bárbara would react when she learned that the young woman she trusted to live in her house and take care of little Pedro ended up prostituting herself with her adventurous son. What would Carlos' reaction be when he was informed of the madness committed by his daughter, how would he react to such shame? What to say to Patricia who had the cadence to warn her of such great danger?

Tell you that by not considering your warnings you were in that terrible situation? Certainly, she would be expelled from there with no right to anything they were powerful people and nothing would stop them from tiptoeing her out of the mansion would he return to his mother's house? Would she be ready and willing to bow her head and listen to her screams throwing her face that was in fact a failure, a daughter's drug that only served to cause problems.

And bring shame on the family? What was he going to say to the younger sister who begged her to be careful and not do anything crazy? How to face the envious neighbors who saw their financial growth and gnawed at the inside because their children were not so lucky, who would now laugh at his fall and stomp on his financial and moral bankruptcy?

It was lost, it fell from the edge like an arrow towards the bottom of the deepest pit. She felt that a seed germinated inside her womb, a fetus was forming, a life would soon be ready to come into the world and she, in turn, would not have the slightest condition to receive it, nor to offer the care and comfort you would need so much.

The days passed. After the conversation they had that morning, both Joana and Dr. Patricia started to monitor the young woman's behavior inside the house as if they were trying to confirm their suspicions. If in fact she and Luciano had any kind of involvement, the sequels would appear sooner or later.

Something as serious as an unwanted pregnancy would be most likely, since he left without even saying goodbye to his sister and the housekeeper, whom he seemed to consider. As a doctor, Patricia was well aware of physical changes in people

And day after day Nathalia appearance was visible, her behavior suspicious, whenever she was present at the mansion, she realized that the girl seemed to want to escape her presence, as if she avoided being analyzed from the perspective of the experienced professional.

But fate is canny, purposeful and vindictive. He leads us on paths never before known, he lifts us up and then he makes us fall. It tests our capacity to the last thousandth of forces.

Puts us in various types of labyrinths and only reaches out to get rid of death if we realize that we will not be able to get out of the hole where we were thrown without your help. Life is his story he writes with a pen and gold ink. We are the characters of this novel that he creates and allows us to live in this world, this earth and planet.

In this theater each person in particular is born with a role to act on that stage, as an important part in the existential context that this same destiny gives rise to. We are your guinea pigs, your dolls, your toys. The character lived by Nathalia do Valle brought in her baggage the sad mission of being consumed by ambition and the desire to be someone important at any cost. And from what you could see, the price was terrible.

On a Friday morning, the young woman took care of little Pedro, the autistic boy, when she fell to the ground before the surprised looks of the child who, for not understanding what would be happening to her companion, started to scream desperately, drawing the attention of the other employees who came to your aid.

Dr. Patricia received a phone call from Joana in her clinic that reported what had happened and asked for instructions on how to proceed in the face of the serious situation, when she was instructed that the driver take the girl in a hurry to be treated urgently in the place that was nearby. After some exams the doctor proved what she feared beforehand, Nathalia was four weeks pregnant.

He expected a child from his inconsequential brother. There was the explanation for why he had left for Paris. With no further loss of time, she met with her parents in the late afternoon and passed on information on the patient's real condition, without hiding the full certainty that the child was a Mendes, the result of another of Luciano's inconsequential sexual relations with the maids.

76

As he has always done since his adolescence, In fact, that boy's insane attitude had already become frequent.

— We cannot allow Luciano to continue abusing the girls who come to work in this house, we have to put an end to this situation, until when will this persist without taking a position contrary to my brother's lack of character?

— And what do you want us to do, Patricia, to force our son to marry a poor girl like that just because she expects a child with our blood? What is at stake here is not only to repair Luciano's possible error, but the future of all our assets, to allow the birth of this child is to make him the heir of an incalculable fortune and this cannot be allowed to happen.

— Possible error? Do you think there is the slightest possibility that this maid's pregnancy is any other than my brother's? Who would be so irresponsible here? Of course, this son belongs to Luciano, my father, the room that surely you and mom intend to keep the girl aborting to hide the irresponsibility of that kid!

— Abortion of the fetus is the best solution in these cases of an unwanted pregnancy, you as a doctor should know that

— Yes, I know very well and I even agree if it is a case of rape. But in this case, it was with the full consent of the two, that poor girl trusted the false promises of love of that scoundrel! This time I will not be part of or agree with this little shame, my opinion is that we bring Luciano back to assume his actions

— But no way, my son will not marry this slum! Damn time when I admit this girl to work in our house

— Mom, forgive me for being so frank in my words, but you and Dad are the biggest culprits for Luciano's immoral addiction…

Always running his hands over his head when he does something crazy

— Your brother since he was a little boy, is a bit of a problem, and our role as parents is to help him overcome his moral failures until he matures and becomes firm in life.

— At what cost, in Dona Barbara? To the detriment of the life and happiness of these poor girls who fall for that bastard's speech?

— Luciano is our son and his brother, we must always be by his side, regardless of the situation in which he finds himself, never on the opposite side

— You are completely wrong, my mother, we must stand on the right side, defend what is right!

— And what seems right for you at this moment, Patricia, to share everything we have struggled for decades to build with a gun that was given to your brother, aiming to get along in life? Don't you realize that this girl is only interested in our money?

— Ah, yes Dad, I had forgotten what is the only thing this family considers important, the damned Mendes money!

— A money considered cursed by you, my daughter, but which has supported your studies in the biggest and best medical schools abroad, has enabled you today to become a great businesswoman, owner of your own clinic and to be this shining woman in which you are. became

— Yes, and I have to say that I am grateful for all that you have given me. But even so I will not be conniving with such a lack of character, enough of throwing my brother's barbaric mistakes into neglect, causing damage to the lives of so many innocent women

— Innocent? Do you consider innocence a girl who surrenders on the tray to the son of a millionaire in the hope of making a fortune? Or does it perhaps believe that in the middle of the 20th century there are still girls who are completely innocent in their purposes?

— The way you think and act both disgusts me!

With this statement, Patricia leaves the room where she confronted her parents for the way they put warm cloths, on her brother's attitudes and leaves a heavy atmosphere in the air, which would lead the Mendes to take an immediate position in the face of yet another of the many confusions created by their son older, against his maids.

— Everything is repeated, until when are we going to plug the moral holes dug by Luciano?

— Until he matures, Edgar, he is our son and needs all our support to overcome this flaw in his character

— I only wonder how long we will have to be serving as support for this unscrupulous kid without changing a single millimeter in his attitudes.

— Until he finally gets it, what we can't do is give up on him

— And these poor girls that we buy the silence of the families and the abortions that we force to do in order to free him from bigger complications, how are they? And if it were our daughter, Barbara, would we agree with so much impunity?

— Please do not compare these riverside rivers with no future with our daughter. Patricia was made from another type of clay, a special and unique ceramic, belongs to another world.

Occupies another level in life and would never commit a vulgar act like this. These girls open their legs to the first person who appears and then claim correction for their mistakes. We are not going to sacrifice our assets or our son's future because of these bitches' ambition

— And now, what will be the next step to cover up this scandal caused by that bastard?

— Don't refer to him that way, Edgar, remember who he inherited such a lack of character

— In fact, in my youth I was doing some, but not as much as he is, he is crossing the line

— Don't be ironic with me, because I just wasn't one of your objects of pleasure anymore because I made myself smart and held the brim of your hat until you married me, in addition to my family members threatened you with death to the point of your parents giving in. to accept me in the family. Regardless of the almost fatal shot that my father took, through which he almost descends to the city of feet together, which convinced old Mendes to agree to our marriage

— Okay, okay, I recognize that I gave our son that damned inheritance received from my ancestors, all Mendes abused domestic workers and that became tradition in the family. But I think you should avoid this comment, because nobody here knows of its mediocre origin, not even our children

— And they won't even know, that would make fun of me in the face of society and my employees. No one can know that I came from the mud like so many others. We must act immediately, before the girl's pregnancy becomes visible.

— I will take the necessary measures, immediately!

The couple ends the conversation and Edgar retires to his quarters, while Barbara goes looking for Joana, who had overheard part of the conversation between the bosses and hurriedly headed for the kitchen, disguising her curiosity. It was still possible for her to hear her employer's statements to her husband as to the fact that she came from humble origins, as well as all of her employees, and this perplexed her.

— Patricia!

— Yes, missus

— I need to pass you some tasks, sit here

— Yes, missus

— You have lived in this house for many years and have become a person of our most complete confidence, followed the trajectory of this family and are aware of many of our secrets

— Certainly, Dona Barbara

— Very well, then you will have to know and keep one more of them, we hope to be able to count on your total discretion

— You can be calm about that, missus

— Our boy committed another great prank, Joana, and as always, we will have to clean up all the dirt left by him

— Holy God, Dona Barbara, another pregnant maid?

— Yes, and this time it will affect one of our oldest employees

— Oh, my Christ, the Carlos?

— Yes, unfortunately your daughter acted recklessly and ended up falling for Luciano, she is one month pregnant and we need to cancel this pregnancy as soon as possible. So, I will have to dismiss both father and daughter, so that there is no root of this sad episode in the mansion

— It is a great pity, because he is a hardworking, helpful and reliable man

— I know that much more than you, Joana, but we can't do anything else. We will talk to him and his daughter, propose the abortion and, as usual, pay a good amount of money to the family. Then dismiss them

— Leave it, missus, I already know exactly how things should be. I will talk to Carlos and I will reveal to you everything that is happening, don't worry

— Okay, do it as soon as possible and then let me know the exact time to reach an agreement with the employee and the girl

— Yes ma'am

Chapter Four - The Bottom of the Well

— Carlos, we need to have a very serious conversation, come with me here in the kitchen to have coffee

— My goodness, woman, talking like that makes me scared, what happened?

— Come soon, man, then you will know what it is!

After being seated at one of the tables in the room, Joana, intends to make the porter aware of the bad news, but does not quite know where to start and keeps going around, until the impatient man shows some irritation.

— Hurry up, woman, stop all the bullshit and talk at once about why you called me here!

— Okay, so here we go: The boss wants to talk to you in the meeting room, the big one at the end of the hall

— I know where it is, but what is it about?

— Calm man, don't worry, look at that heart

— If you continue with all this suspense, I might end up having a heart attack

— Something very serious happened here in the mansion that involves your daughter

— Don't tell me that tomboy dared to disrespect his boss or boss, did he catch something hidden or do some other crazy thing?

— More or less!

— Jesus Christ, so tell me right away, woman, don't torture me more than I can handle!

— It's related to Doctor Luciano you know what I mean?

Carlos worked there for a long time to know the boy's bad reputation. He was aware of his shameful practices and the protection that the bosses gave to the troublemaker, as soon as Joana started the details about what happened, he understood without needing any further details about the seriousness of the situation, his daughter was yet another victim of the unfortunate.

— My God, how could such a disgrace happen soon to my girl, Joana?

— I'm sorry, my friend, but the truth is that it happened and she is four weeks pregnant. She looks shabby, pale, thinner ... Didn't you notice that there was something wrong with the girl, Carlos?

— To be honest, I'm not one to observe and pay much attention to these details

— Well know that this is a terrible mistake, our daughters must be monitored daily to avoid this type of surprises

— Now I understand why this month she did not want to spend the day off at home.

— And now, what are you going to do?

— I will face the situation, talk to the mistress and see what solution she will give to all this, my daughter is still a minor and Mrs. Luciano will have to assume what he did, it will not come cheap with me as it happened with the other parents who downloaded the head and were at the loss

— Actually, Carlos, the bosses bought their silence for a good amount

— How is it, Joana, by any chance is this kind of proposal that the boss wants to make me? Do you think I'm going to negotiate a daughter's honor?

— I think that is exactly her intention, my friend, to pay for your silence

— Because this time she will listen, because I am not that kind of naughty father who takes bribes, I have dignity my friend

— So, the message has already been given, now go talk to Mrs. Debora at the place I told you about, she is waiting for you

— Call the girl for me, please

— The mistress has nothing to talk to your daughter, the conversation is just between the two of you. But I give you an advice, old friend, try to restrain yourself and don't forget that you are inside her house, that these people are powerful and facing them is dangerous

— Do not think it will scare me, she will hear what no other father had the courage to tell her

That father felt in his mouth the bitterness of disappointment that his most beloved daughter caused him with his act of madness, he never thought that his wife would be right to warn him of the risks he would run.

By putting Nathalia inside his workplace, but even so he would allow himself to be so shamefully humiliated by a woman whose character was similar to that of her son, as she bribed her victims to keep him free of the deserved punishments. His intention was to make the miserable man pay for that and all the other abuses he committed against women who blindly trusted his charms.

— Make yourself comfortable, Mr. Carlos, sit down! If you're here, it's because Joana has already let you know about the situation, so let's get to the point. Tell me how I can compensate you for the damage that my son's irresponsible has caused your girl, I am sure we will enter into a fair agreement for you and your family

— You are correct in one thing, Dona Barbara, I am already well informed about what happened. However, he made a serious mistake if he imagined that my presence here is to accept any form of bribery. Contrary to what you might imagine, I may not have the fortune that this family has, but I have dignity and I do not negotiate the honor of my daughters.

— We will not be able to repay the honor of your daughter, Mr. Carlos, at most we can reward you with good financial help

— It would be more, fair to hold your child responsible for what you did

— Forcing you to marry a girl who doesn't belong to the same social class as his? Who doesn't have the minimum of attributes to be part of this family or to become the mother of our grandchildren? Look at you and your family and be aware of the huge social differences that exist on both sides. Realize that Luciano's union with his daughter wouldn't even be possible

— Very well, you are absolutely right, your observation is correct.

But, why didn't he analyze these details and all these differences before going to bed with Nathalia? If a girl like her doesn't fit to be the wife of a Mendes, why did her son choose to find pleasure right away with a favela, whose father is an employee of that house and everyone knows our financial condition? A millionaire as he is, why didn't he try to satisfy his desires with a princess from high society, whose level was equal to or higher than his? Is it because for crooks like your child, poor women are disposable?

— That only he could answer you, the reason we have this conversation is another

— No, you're wrong. I didn't come here to accept your immoral proposal, your bribe, shut up. I'm here, Dona Bárbara, to give you a single warning: I will take my girl home the way she is, as I will not allow her to be taken to a clandestine clinic, as was done with the others, for a criminal abortion. But one thing's for sure, if one day that son of a bitch gets back on his feet in this city and I know about it, he will be accountable to me for the harm done to my girl

—Are you by any chance threatening my son, your Carlos?

— No lady, I'm not the type to make threats, this is a warning. Tell Doctor Luciano to stay there in France and never return, because if he comes back or marries my daughter and takes over the child or he will have to settle accounts with me. You can be sure of that!

— Get out of my house right now and take your daughter along, I don't want to see you around here anymore!"

— We will do that, but not before you pay us everything you owe us, or I will report you right now for coercion and bribery to the authorities

— Don't waste your time on this nonsense, you won't get anything against us

— I know that, with the power you have I would buy all the justice of that State, but your name is worth a lot to be involved in a great scandal, don't you think?

— Okay, I'll have your labor rights accounted for along with the girl's and we'll let you know the day you come to get your money, now give me the pleasure of never seeing you again. If you don't want to be compensated for the damage done to your daughter, leave my house!

— I will do that, but don't forget the recommendations made to your son, ask him never to return to this city!

— Out! Get out of that house immediately!

Carlos takes care of the insensitive woman's ordinances and when he goes down, he already finds the teenager with her bags ready in the mansion's courtyard, he looked her in the eyes and made clear his immense disappointment. problems against the boss who hurriedly expelled the two of them from there.

At the same moment they left the mansion, they found Patricia vehicle that had just arrived at the place. Upon getting out of her car in the large parking lot, the doctor understood immediately what was going on and went to the housekeeper to check if her assessments of what she saw would be correct.

— What happened here, Joana, because Mr. Carlos and his daughter were leaving, did my mother reach the extreme of injustice?

To the point of blaming the poor man for his daughter's mistakes?

- And what did you expect to happen, Patricia? You know very well that the boss thinks she can solve everything with money.

So, she called the man up there and proposed to pay for the damage done by her brother, right? But apparently the girl's father refused to accept shut up, they argued and she told them to leave the mansion as soon as possible.

— Don't worry, Joana, I know you heard their conversation, tell me everything

— So, my daughter, it got really hot there!

— What do you mean, hot? Be clearer, woman!

— Your Carlos threatened to take revenge on Luciano! He said it was for the mistress to warn her son that if he returns to Belem, he will have to take on the girl Nathalia and the child or he will see him

— Look, I know that my brother was irresponsible and deserves the beauty of a punishment, but making threats is a crime, nobody can go around threatening anyone's life

— Tell that to a father who saw his teenage daughter being used and then discarded by an adventurous kid, leaving behind a grandson to raise

— I know that, Joana, it really isn't easy. You know what, I'm not going to stay here defending my bastard brother or a girl to warn of the danger and I didn't want to consider my advice. Both were wrong and are worthy of punishment, so pay for your errors.

— And I'll take care of my chores!

Finally, the worst moment of Nathalia life was very close to happening. Father and daughter enter the narrow street where they lived, the scene was quite different from the previous ones, when he arrived in big cars and accompanied by playboys. Now, the neighbors would start to criticize instead of simple gossip.

The girl who left the favela and started to live in a mansion seemed to have done badly and was returning home after the visible failure. With a small suitcase in one hand, bags in the other and a heavy backpack on her back, the teenager followed her head down the street in the company of Carlos, whose face showed the bitter air of disappointment, anyone who saw her countenance could imagine that something terrible was happening to her. it had happened.

As he passed in front of the snack car he was greeted, but he paid no attention, if any neighbor paid off in any way, he was able to notice. When he arrived in front of his residence he knocked and the door soon opened. It was a surprise to his wife and youngest daughter that they were there exactly during working hours and especially Nathalia, who lived at work. For Luiza it was a bad sign, a terrible thing would have happened.

— What happened, why are they here at this time? And that pile of luggage, what does that mean?

— Stop with so many questions, woman, at least let us finish entering this blessed house!

Nathalia looks at Christina and, after releasing the weight of her hands, she hugs her crying, this attitude made her mother realize what had happened.

— My God, I do not believe, what I feared most must have happened ... This girl did something stupid and they sent them both away from work! Was that it, Carlos?

— I don't even tell you, woman, what you warned me about when I decided to take this tomboy to the mansion was fulfilled to the letter!

The young woman remained standing, her head bowed and crying. Christina stared at her sister as if reproving her mistake. After all, both warned her to be careful. The mother, in turn, began to slap her daughter all over her body and hit her hard on the face. For the first time she did that and Carlos did not move an inch to try to contain it.

— Miserable, I knew it would happen! Always causing us problems, causing confusion and shaming the family wherever they go!

— Oh, mom, stop it! Don't hit me, mom!

— I should beat you was with that broom handle, you clumsy one, to teach you how to take a turn in life!

The young woman took the biggest and hardest spanking of her life and the martyrdom ended only when the woman finally got tired of imposing the punishment on her daughter. The father went up to the couple's room to avoid watching the cruel spectacle, he loved that girl in the depths of his soul and preferred that his wife give him the appropriate punishment, as he would not have the courage.

Her heart was beating fast as she heard Luiza's screams still bursting with hatred for what the teenager did and worried when she finally knew that the worst hadn't yet been revealed to her: That her daughter was pregnant. Surely, she would not react well to this type of news.

— Now get out of my way while I'm still recognizing you as a daughter. Get out of here!

Nathalia receives help from her sister to gather her belongings and goes up to her room…

Luiza also goes up right afterwards and goes to her rooms in search of further explanations with her husband

— Now it is you who will finish telling me this story, Carlos, what really happened? Tell me soon, man, because I lack patience! What did that fret do for you two to be thrown out of service?

— The worst thing in the world ...

— Did she disrespect her bosses, hurt someone, steal from the mansion ...? Come on, man, for God's sake, just open that mouth and tell me!

— Calm down, woman, control yourself! This hysteria did not see to solve our problems that are now bigger than before

— Bigger? So, for you to talk like that, what that crazy woman must have done was really terrible! Spill it out, boy, what's so bad this girl has been doing?

— Our daughter ended up getting involved with a little playboy, son of the boss

— How is it, Carlos, all this confusion just because your daughter's rascal could not see a male in front of her?

— Our daughter, Luiza!

— Wow, since this girl was born, she was always more yours than mine. Do you forget that you gave her more protection than she really deserved? Now there is the result of all that freshness with the daughter of the heart!

— Get ready, there's more ...

— Then say it all at once, slow man!

— Our daughter slept with that guy, got lost with him, that's it!

— How is it, Carlos, that slut went to bed with a male inside the house where she worked?

— And the most absurd was not yet, she is pregnant with the bastard!

Luiza turned red with hatred and her explosive temper turned it into a bomb capable of exploding at any second and despite the man's efforts to contain it, nothing held her back. She left in a rage towards Christina's room, where her oldest daughter was being comforted by her sister.

— So much so that I told you to be careful, because you never listen to people's advice?

— I do not know, my sister, it seems that it is my curse just to choose wrong ways in life

— Wow, Nathalia, even your sister-in-law told you that Cara was a profiteer and even then, you still fell for him?

— I really am a tremendous idiot!

— As for that I have to admit, it is being very stupid, see?

— I deserve this!

Suddenly the door to the room is punched with fists and kicks, on the other side there was a distraught woman.

— Chris, open that door!

— Calm down, mom, what's up now?

— Open the damn door or it'll be left for you too!

The door opens and is invaded by the furious mother who angrily went after Nathalia, kicking her and beating her face with immense revolt.

— Calm mother, leave her!

— Get out of here, Christina, leave me!

— Stop, Luiza, you can cause an abortion in the girl!

— What is this story about abortion, who is pregnant!

— That bitch of your sister, she got the boss's son!

Luiza continued to beat her daughter, her face was becoming disfigured from so many slaps and the rest of her body suffered from kicks. At that time, there was no statute that could protect minors from physical aggression practiced by their parents, so what the neighbors could do was hear the screams of a poor girl and hope that she could escape that sabbatical from almost endless blows. Finally, luckily for her, Carlos dresses up as a man and decides to put order in the house.

— Enough, Luiza, now you're crossing the line!

— What moral do you have to want to determine when I should stop punishing this dirty bitch? After all, didn't you always defend this useless dog?

At that moment he seems to have decided to completely change his usual role as a coward to take a more authoritarian position in the family. This role played for several years by his wife, who always gave the last word on everything. Thus, as soon as he finished hearing Luiza's affront and it was soon giving his wife a strong turn of hand over her face that she was thrown in the corner of the nearest wall. The two girls were paralyzed with fright when they saw their father taking that violent attitude against their mother, it was the first time that they witnessed such a scene.

But the woman was an irreducible type, persistent in her authoritarian stance, and went on to face-to-face confrontation with her husband. Leaving, however, with the worst. She took another slap in the face and was thrown back to the place from which she dared to rise, it would have been better to accept her condition as more fragile and quiet down. Christina comes to your protection.

— Mom, be quiet!

— Miserable, I'm going to kill you!

— Take it easy mom!

— All because of that bitch!

Carlos leaves the room back and Nathalia remains lying on the bed completely hurt, Luiza before retiring expresses to her daughter a little more of her contempt.

— Damn time I spawned you inside me, you filth!

Her mother's words were like a sharp blade that cut through her, bleeding terribly from her already suffering heart. Only the two sisters remained in the place, after the sad episode. Gradually she catches her breath and starts talking to her sister.

— You must be hating me, right?

— No, just disappointed. How did you get to that? Did you see what your selfish attitude did?

— What do you mean, what are you talking about? I was not selfish!

— Do you think you fool me, Nathalia? I know very well that you went to bed with the little playboy thinking about getting along with him. He lives wanting to hold a man by the belly, wanting to get rich easy!

Did you happen to think that beauty holds man, your beast?

— Now you want to step on me too?

— Mom is right, you are a big delay for this family!

— Chris, don't talk to me like that, isn't it enough that the spanking Mom gave me?

— It was still not enough, just calm things down and you will make another mistake! Now give me some time to go down and see how my mom is doing

Christina was spoiled and treated by Luiza as if she were a porcelain doll, her attachment to her was notorious for everyone, but when she went down the stairs what she saw were new aggressions between her parents. Carlos and his wife were still arguing when they went from verbal aggression to physical, they got together and knocked everything over the room.

— Stop it now, you two! Are you crazy?

Nathalia hears her sister's screams, trying to separate the two who attacked each other, goes down and tries to help. Nathan, the youngest son, arrives and tries to calm them down. The situation became untenable, the older daughter's attitude destroyed not only her father's professional life, but his relationship with his wife. His acts of complete madness have collapsed in a definitive relationship that survived by a thread.

The spirits were very high, the two girls tried to contain each side and the boy stood between the distance that separated them. A macabre silence hung in the house, a dark cloud seemed to be dissipating in the room, after the truce between the two gladiators. There one could see the words of Christ being fulfilled by stating that a man's worst enemy will come out of his own home.

Of those closest to him. That couple never lived a great love story, she held her partner by the belly, through an unwanted pregnancy. He, remained by his side and agreed to form that family for the love of the daughter who had been born, bet that it could work.

Luiza hated Nathalia from the bottom of her soul, because she was like a mirror, showing the cowardly act she committed against her husband, when she used it in bad faith and through that child forced him to assume a relationship where no drop of love existed.

And now when he saw her making the same mistakes as her youth, she burst into anger, she was seeing herself in her daughter's attitudes and that left her full of sorrows and remorse, ashamed of herself.

The blows made on the teenager were as if they were on her own body, deep down she knew that she was the one who deserved it all, but as she would not be able to beat herself, she struck the blows on her image and likeness. After that sad episode there was a lull, Christina lets Brother Nathan know about everything and the rest of the day went by without any major problems.

In his chambers, Carlos remains lying down to reflect on all that terrible situation, when suddenly he feels strong pressure in his chest, shortness of breath and dizziness. He gets up with great difficulty and goes to the room where the two daughters were, in search of help. Knocking on the door insistently, Chris opens it in fright, thinking he is again the mother who decided to punish his sister.

But he is faced with his father who, unable to keep up, falls at his feet, fainting.

— Dad!? My God, Nathalia run here!

— Dad! Dad! Call the ambulance, Chris, quickly!

— Mom! Hurry up here!

— May I know what the hell is going on? Oh my God, Carlos! What happened?

— We don't know, he knocked on the door here and when we opened, he fell passed out!

— We need to get him to the hospital fast!

— Chris is calling the ambulance!

After a few moments, the public ambulance 192 arrives and health professionals take the patient to the nearest hospital, after an accurate diagnosis, the family members are informed that Carlos had been the victim of a serious heart attack and needed to remain hospitalized. Upon returning home, Luiza began to harass her daughter again and blame her for everything bad that was happening to her father.

— All your fault, unhappy!

— Mom, please!

— Stay out of this Christina!

— My God, when will this mess end here?

— When that bastard has heard enough!

— It is not enough that my father is almost dead, prostrate in a hospital because of all this confusion?

— Ask your sister, she started it all!

- Okay, I was wrong, but who is the lady to point the finger at me?

Did I not just follow your example, Dona Luiza? Wasn't it the lady who arrested my father with a belly? What are you complaining about? I learned from you, Mom!

The daughter's attitude left the woman hysterical, started towards the teenager with a bright flame of hatred in her eyes, but was restrained by Christina, who despite being younger than her sister was physically stronger and able to prevent the mother's action

. — Let her come, Chris, let her beat me until I can erase the image that I represent before her eyes from her mind. The kind of little woman unable to win a man's heart without playing dirty like only she knew how to do with our father, that's why she hates me, doesn't she, Mom?

— You damn, unhappy!

— Yes, I am unhappy, because I was damned lucky to be your daughter!

Nathalia goes up and remains reclusive in her room for the rest of the day. Hourly Christina called the hospital to hear from her father, which was not always possible. After calming the mother, the sister goes to her.

— My God, what a depressing situation this is!

— Didn't you have to go to college today?

— And how to do this with all this confusion here at home? Look at Dad's situation!

— Sorry, sis, it wasn't my intention to disrupt your studies

— Oh no? And what did you think would happen when you decided to go to bed with that bastard?

— That would do me good

— To get along? A slum with a Millionaire? Are you crazy for good?

— I believe it can still work today

— I know, believing in fairy tales is tremendous stupidity!

— Okay, that's what I am for you in this house, a donkey!

— And it's not? Isn't being pregnant with an adventurer a tremendous idiot, my sister?

The two were still talking about the latest events, when the landline that had been installed a few days ago and that could have canceled the line due to lack of payments, due to the unemployment of those who bought it rang. It sounds insistently on the extension on the living room shelf and the two will answer.

— Hello, are you from the hospital?

— Yes, are you related to Patient Carlos dos Santos Cunha?

— Yes, I am his eldest daughter, how is my father?

— Good night, we are calling to ask a family member to come immediately to the hospital

— But what happened to him, how is my father?

— Sorry, we are not authorized to give you more information over the phone, come to the hospital and you will have further clarification on the patient's real health status

— Okay, I'll do it

— What they said?

— They said they can only tell us about Dad's situation if we go there in person

— More than hell!

— Come on, we need to know what's going on with him

Arriving at the hospital, the two sisters were taken to speak to a social worker in a separate room. With that, the girls began to fear the worst, became worried and waited for bad news. The tall, blond woman, with yellow eyes and a serious face, greets them and does not use half words, cruelly goes straight to the point.

- Good night, my name is Luciana and I am the social worker of this unit, unfortunately I was sent here to inform you of the death of Mr. Carlos dos Santos Cunha, admitted today in this hospital victimized by a heart attack

— There, my God, it can't be true!

— No! My dad!

— We're sorry. The body needs to be recognized and then released to proceed with the referral to the Expert Center and the release of the body to family members. Are both able to do these procedures or do you think it is convenient to call another family member?

— No, leave it alone, I'll do it myself

— Very well, please follow me

— Wait here, Chris, I'll be right back

— Okay, I'll take it and call mom

— Do it

Christina went to inform her mother about what happened…

And Nathalia recognized her father's body, it was not easy to see him stretched out in that refrigerator, his face swollen, his lips purple, his eyes closed and without that gleam in his eyes always ready to understand. Not only did he lose his father, but his only and best friend.

Now, more than ever, she was alone in the world, there was nothing left for her but the child she was waiting for, perhaps she would find in him the support she needed to be happy. The funeral was taking place at the house, a lot of sadness was stamped on the faces of family members and all those present, the neighbors gave their condolences to the widow and the dead man's children, it was the last farewell of the one who once sacrificed his own happiness in favor of a family. devastated by that tragedy.

As soon as the coffin with the body was removed by the funeral home, everyone headed towards Park of the Palms, a private cemetery where, despite having a low salary, Carlos, when in life, bought a grave and started paying the funeral plan. Even in the face of so much disgrace, at least a decent burial the deceased could have.

The return home took place under a blanket of revolt on the part of the brothers and relatives, since everyone was informed in what circumstances everything happened, they were unanimous in blaming Nathalia for the death of the father. Two days passed and Luiza calls her daughter for a serious and definitive conversation.

— Come here, we need to talk

— What is it, mother?

— Do not call me mother, after all that caused us I do not allow you that right!

— But you are my mother, how can I address you in another way?

— Find a way! But let's get to it: It won't be possible for the two of us to continue living together in this house, I can't tolerate looking at that cynical face of yours. So, I want to ask you to leave here and take that filthy child that you got from that scoundrel!

— Good heavens, mother, don't do this to me! Where am I going?

— I have no idea, turn around!

The youngest daughter went down the stairs to the living room, where the two were talking, and she still heard her sister's plea not to be expelled by her mother, showing solidarity in favor of her.

— What is it, mom, you can't put the mana out of the house in this state, she is pregnant!

— If you are not satisfied with my decision go with her, the decision has already been made and here this criminal is no longer!

— How, criminal, if I never killed anyone?

— Are you crazy, mom, what nonsense is this?

— That one was the one who caused your father's death, if he hadn't done all the madness, he did he would still be alive and among us. She's a killer, yes!

Nathalia cries breathlessly, Christina tries to calm her down and at the same time scolds her mother's behavior, however, she knows that if Dona Luiza decided the thing would have to be done. Take the sister to the bedroom and let her relieve the pain through the tears that run down her face, then put the reality before her eyes.

— Yeah, my sister, it got really hard for you. And now, what do you want to do?

— Do not know...

— But you need to find a way out because mommy doesn't want you here anymore and she knows that if Dona Luiza makes a decision against someone it is for real and she won't go back, especially if it is not with the person's face, as in your case

— Yes, I know

— And then, woman, how will it be?

— Are you also pressing me to leave soon?

— Yes, I am, because I know that if I don't do this as soon as possible, our mother will go to violence with you, she may even throw your things in the middle of the street. You know how she is, sis, and daddy is no longer here to defend you

— Okay, Chris, you're absolutely right. There is no use trying to convince my mother that she is wrong to do this to me. I think I'll ask for shelter at Uncle Chico's house for a while, until I see what I do with my life

— I don't know if he will want to help you, Dad's whole family is mad at you because Mom made up their mind

— No, the uncle was always my friend, I know he will want to help me

— Well, you know. But if it doesn't work try our other relatives, now go quickly and when you have a place to stay come and get your things

— Okay, so I'm going

— I wish you luck

The young goes, in search of protection at the relatives' homes, the first to be visited was Francisco, owner of the snack cart where he used to go in the company of his father, he had in mind that he would be well accepted, as he showed a lot of affection for her.

— We are sorry, my niece, but here at home the family is very large and we are mostly unemployed, I support the house alone with snacks, it is not possible to increase mouths to feed. Try your other uncles, my daughter!

— Okay, Uncle Chico, sorry for the inconvenience

Lucia was a little absent aunt, but a good person, as well as a fervent Catholic. No doubt she would have your support, as she was a very welcoming woman. She was Luiza's sister, but less bitter.

— Come on, my dear, I really learned what happened even though I didn't go to your father's funeral, I know it's not being easy for the family. As for your request to stay here with me, unfortunately it will not be possible to attend, baby, because I am used to living alone, in my corner, having my privacy ... You know, I never had children and I will not adapt to sharing my space with someone else. I'm sorry, but it won't work. Visit your other relatives, you will surely find one of them that can give you shelter, I cannot.

Everyone decided to close the doors for the young woman, as they were always against the way she was protected by the parent. The mother's relatives had a certain envy of the man's love for her daughter, while those on her father's side despised her for knowing that it was through her that Luiza blackmailed Carlos to be trapped in that relationship with no future. She knocked on the door of several relatives.

But none proposed to help her, they all remained closed. Finally, he thought of his friend Virginia, who looked more like a sister and lived very close to her home and knew of her suffering, although she thought it strange that she had not even come to offer her condolences for her father's death. There, the disappointment could not have been worse.

— Look, my friend is sorry, but my mom didn't agree to let me stay here at home, she doesn't want to get in trouble with the neighbor. You know how she is she loves a shack and we don't want to get involved in scandals

— Talk to your mother that it's only for a while until my son is born and I look for my way

— Gee, I'm really sorry, see? But it won't work, my mother made it very clear that she can't help

The one who pretended to be your best friend knocks on the door and leaves the poor girl aimlessly and aimlessly on the same street where they once played and had fun together. Completely lost and not knowing which way to go, she returned home and told her sister about the desperate situation in which she found herself.

— I'm screwed, my sister, everyone knocked on my face, I don't know what to do or where to go

— I told you it wasn't going to be easy to count on the help of our relatives, both from Mom and Dad, they hate you

— My God, Chris, do I really deserve so much contempt?

— And now, how will it be? Here you can't stay

- Look, sis, keep my things there...

And I'll go out for a while, maybe walking I think better and find a way out

— Walk where, my sister?

— I don't know, street outside

Nathalia took a drive with some spare change and went to the shopping center, in Presidente Vargas square, located in the most privileged area of the city, sat down on one of the several banks there and was wondering what to do. Her pregnancy reached the middle of the second month and the belly was more visible.

After at least an hour standing in the same place, sitting under a tall mango laden with fruit, she was surprised by the fall of several of them ripe, due to the strong blowing of the winds.

The fright was immense and he was ill, he saw everything revolving around him, but someone came to his protection. She was a young lady who passed by the place and realized what had happened, took the trouble to see her looking ill and was willing to help her.

— Okay? I couldn't help noticing the scare you took and it seems that you are pregnant?

— Ah yes, thank you very much!

— No need to thank me, I'm just doing a good deed. Are you waiting for someone?

— Not really. I'm trying to find an answer

— I did not understand

— Well, never mind, it's my thing, thanks again for the help

— You don't really want to open up with me, I'm walking here in the square, I live nearby and decided to come and spend time. Wouldn't you like to come over to my apartment for some juice, tea or something while we talk?

She was tired, hungry and this was a great opportunity to feed herself, after all, she didn't even have another coin to return home, if that was possible after she was expelled by her mother. It seemed that destiny wanted to reach out to him and would not act arrogantly or proud at such a delicate moment in his life.

— Yes, I do

— So come on, I'm looking forward to getting to know each other better. My name is Suellen, nice to meet you

— I'm Nathalia, the pleasure is all mine

Together with their new friend, they went to the other side of the square, on Ó de Almeida Street, where the Prado Monteiro building was located, a luxury condominium where Suellen Costa, a successful lawyer, lived. After making a whimsical snack prepared by Edna, the maid, the two started to talk in comfortable armchairs in the large room. The owner of that beautiful apartment, whose fifth floor balcony overlooked Guajara Bay, was thrilled to hear the whole sad story of the poor girl who, dreaming of a better life and believing in the certainty of her first love, ended up giving herself to the wrong man.

The death of the father, her only friend, the way she was treated cowardly by the mother, her expulsion from home, the rejection by family members and the child that was developing in her womb without any preparation and medical monitoring, the former employer who , being a renowned millionaire, she refused to pay her labor rights and was not even sure if she would give those of her deceased father.

He talked about everything, Suellen had a degree in criminal law, but she also worked as a public defender in the labor area and decided to buy the fight, made herself available to the young woman to defend her cause and demand compensation for the moral damages suffered, because no one can be above the law, even that has very high economic and financial power.

Aware that her friend was lying on the street and was rejected by her own family, she went with her to her mother's house to collect her belongings. From that day on she would be her guest, they would live together in the same house and receive all the necessary care during pregnancy.

When the black Hilux entered the same street as before, the girl used to ride with the rich boyfriends she had, the neighborhood went out the door. They were curious to know who it was, as they would never imagine being the porter's daughter again, as she would have fallen to the bottom of the well, until she was expelled from her home by her mother.

It was a few seconds of expectation on the part of the most gossipy waiting for the vehicle door to open and finally they could see who the illustrious visitors were. The surprise was immense when they realized that the vehicle stopped in front of Luiza's residence and when they saw the young woman who gets out of the luxurious car and goes to her mother's house.

After a few minutes he returns with all his belongings and re-enters the vehicle, which leaves without any of the onlookers understanding what is actually happening. At the gate of the wall that separated the property from the street, Christina stood, watching her sister's departure, and from the top her mother went out the window of two rooms to say goodbye with the look of her daughter that she once despised.

Nathalia do Valle moved in with Suellen and received all necessary care daily, started prenatal care, won a room of her own and bought all the trousseau for the baby on the way. The lawyer filed a lawsuit against the Mendes and requested labor payments from her client, as well as from her deceased father, was at Luiza's residence several times so that together with her they could claim a good indemnity for the family from Carlos, deceased after his resignation from the mansion.

In the end, the Mendes were forced by the courts to pay all that the lawyer demanded in court, despite many appeals by the wealthy businessmen. the agreement for the girl who was abused by Luciano Mendes to receive a good indemnity for the moral damages suffered was finally accepted by Bárbara, when the defender threatened to make public the process that until then ran in secrecy.

For fear of defamation before society, having a name to watch over, he relented. Luiza did very well to be compensated with a very high value and Nathalia received her share. On the first day of that month she was giving birth to a male child, beautiful as his parents. He named him Carlos, in honor of his grandfather and his best friend. Suellen soon stepped forward as a godmother and assured her that her godson would never miss anything, as well as her mother who learned to love as a daughter.

She lived for many years alone, she had only the maid's company and most of her time was divided between work and reading many books, she was addicted to reading. She was married, but widowhood came too soon, taking her great and only love. So, she chose not to give her heart to anyone else, opting for single life. The arrival of Nathalia and little Carlos would be great to fill the emptiness that in a certain way brought in her, since she had no children and was the only heir to a couple of retired judges.

Owners of many goods and properties. However, she visited her parents only occasionally and because she had her own assets, she was not interested in such an inheritance. But now that he had a family before him that God decided to give him, he changed his plans.

— My friend, come here that we have something very important to discuss about your future and my godson's

— No, I'm listening to you, Dona Suellen

— I know how uncomfortable you are to live here without cooperating with expenses, feeling useless, even asked me to give you some work and understand your anguish, after all you are young and want to fight for your independence

— Yes, it's true. I am very grateful for everything you have done for me and my son, but I am not the type who can live that way. From an early age I learned from my father that work brings us dignity, so I confess to being really upset, mainly because I worry about the future of Carlos, because we have everything here, but this wealth belongs to you and not to us. That is, when I leave here, I will have nothing to offer my son

— I fully understand your point of view and respect your way of thinking, as you show character and have no ambitions for what is mine.

— No, never!

— Well, then, I was at my parents' residence earlier today and I was informed by the family doctor that their health is not good. The story of that couple is quite interesting, my friend, they met while still in their teens, dated and married. One was the first love for the other and this relationship continues today, in addition to being the same age and looking like they will leave this life together…

As both were recently diagnosed with cancer

— How interesting, they look like soulmates

— And they really are. But what I need to tell you is that my parents are millionaires, they have an incalculable inheritance that they will leave to me and, as you see, I don't need to, because my late husband and I have built an immense fortune. In fact, I lost sleep thinking about who would be so wealthy if I don't even have children. So today, coming here, it opened my mind and I had an obvious understanding. I saw that I now have heirs, I have you and little Carlos to whom I can leave all this

— My goodness, Dona Suellen, this is too much for us. We can't accept it!

— I know your dignity, my friend, I know I am not interested in my assets.

But I have already decided and this is how things will happen, not just for you, but for the future of my godson

— Okay, if you do that thinking for the sake of my son, I will not be so proud as to refuse such a gesture of love

— So, we are like this, I will provide all the documentation and put you and my godson as my definitive heirs.

And please, from today on, don't call me Mrs. or Madam anymore, will it just be Suellen, agreed? Oh, another thing, we need you to go back to your studies as soon as possible, you need to prepare to manage what you will inherit later and find something to do, in order to feel useful

— I fully agree

With her influence, the lawyer got her friend to take an assessment test…

To verify her learning in the first two years of high school and after several weeks in a preparatory course she took the exam successfully, completed her third year and started college. As her interest was always in becoming a great businesswoman, she opted for Business Administration, a course she completed in just three years of study. While studying, Suellen hired someone to look after little Carlos.

Her efforts and the good performance she showed in college were very pleasing to her friend and helper, who came to the college auditorium to attend her graduation with a strong glow of pride in her eyes. Who was also present there was her sister, Christina, with whom she never stopped communicating and was amazed to see her receive the diploma of graduating at a higher level, when before she detested books Suellen's parents are finally beaten by cancer and go to the other side practically together, one with a difference of days on the other.

Having passed the age of forty, still young, she felt that the burden of managing so much wealth was suffocating her and she immediately passed on her part of the inheritance, still alive, to Nathalia. The girl wisely started to manage all the assets that only increased in number year after year. Throughout this period several things happened, such as the magnificent growth of the son, who at the age of five was a huge and energetic boy, showing as much intelligence as his grandfather.

Nathalia would know how to take advantage of all her intellect, directing him to a bright future so that such knowledge would not be lost like what happened with his father, who despite so much knowledge ended his days working at the entrance of a mansion due to lack of opportunities. Christina completed her studies and was now an NBA physician acquired in the USA, all paid for by her older sister. She achieved her dream of studying abroad and owned her own clinic.

Nathan, after a few ear tugs, devoted himself to his studies and graduated in Mechanical Engineering, followed his sister's advice that warned him that he could be more than just a helper in a car repair shop. To the surprise of the suffering girl who was born in a slum, on the outskirts of the same city where she has now become a successful businesswoman, he and his friend Suellen started dating, despite the age difference, which she did not dare disagree with. Months later they were married and happy.

Final chapter

Even after a long time the atmosphere between mother and daughter was not the best, there still seemed to be a wall that separated one from the other. Several times Nathalia tried to reconnect, gave Luiza everything she needed to have a life of comfort, taking her and her brothers from the favela, placing them in an upscale neighborhood and raising the family's social status.

The mother no longer needed to sew or wash out, nor did she live among those gossips on Hope Street where she was born. The dying daughter, who was expelled from home after making the mistake of believing in her first love, finally realized her dream of becoming an important woman, she has brought that certainty within herself since she was born and understood herself as people in this world, despite your self-confidence seems crazy.

Her name was now among the most important in the city where she was once treated with contempt and injustice. However, not all of this seemed to have made her mother proud, who still despised her with the eyes of someone who would never approve of her being a blessing that the Creator placed in her path. To conquer what seemed impossible, in the end offer you a peaceful and peaceful old age. Over time, the poor girl's wealth in the suburbs multiplied so much that her economic power increased twice as much as that of the Mendes.

Luciano returned from France after a decade and became aware of how evolved the one he used and threw away how to make some garbage, because Sister Patricia herself, now Christina's partner in a network of clinics in the capital, provided her with the information.

He tried several times to reconnect with the intention of meeting his son, but it was in vain, because Nathalia vehemently rejected him, he still felt for the boy a strong attraction, but a part of her despised him for everything bad that made him go through, mainly because of father, for not enduring so much disappointment suffered.

It was a winter morning, when the beautiful woman accompanied her ten-year-old son on his first day of school at Vera Cruz school, the most expensive and important of the time, when he looked up from the wide gate and was faced with a shadow from the past, which reappeared in its present. It was Vinicius, he had married the watery blonde and they had a couple of children who were studying at the same school as Carlos.

Although it has been a long time since they split up, their appearance has not changed much and it has been easy to recognize them both. After accommodating the children in class, the two went to have a drink nearby and caught up.

Deep down, even after all, his passion for Nathalia never dissolved, but she, however, did not feel the same. However, nothing could prevent a good friendship.

In the following years, the beautiful businesswoman remained alone and believed that she would end her days in solitude, dedicating herself to managing her assets. But fate had a surprise reserved for the main character of its history and on a beautiful day, when he decided to go with some friends to a restaurant.

Where they would celebrate an important date, he met Angelo, a very wealthy publicist, intelligent, courteous and widowed, who caused extreme interest. From that friendship came a strong admiration for each other, from this a very fruitful intimate relationship, and, finally, a much more intense passion was born than that felt by Luciano.

Her heart seemed to leap in her chest each time they were together and that warmth allowed all their meetings to be unforgettable. After a night of incomparable love, when there was no longer any doubt as to what they really felt and wanted from each other, he surprises her once again.

— Marry me!

— What did you say?

— Marry me, my love, we will definitely unite our lives!

Without knowing how to contain the enormous emotion she felt at that moment, she gives him the answer she wanted to hear.

— Yes, my love, I wholeheartedly accept to be completely yours!

— I promise to make you happy forever!

— Bobo, by your side I'm already the happiest woman in the world

The couple exchanges kisses and caresses, surrender to each other without fear and a few days later she is entering the Capuchin church, one of the most important in Belem do Pará.

With a crowd of guests, under the sound of traditional wedding music conducted by the Carlos Gomes Orchestra, a yes was said in front of the witnesses and the priest who blessed that happy union.

On the same day, after the reception of the guests at a big party in the mansion where he lived, the bride and groom left for a honeymoon trip in France, a place that he had only heard of before, now he would visit the land where his son's father once lived and imposing proved to be superior.

Now, he was walking the streets of the capital Paris and visited the so-called Eiffel Tower, then returned to Brazil and continued with their lives full of love, peace, happiness and success.

The End

Lightning Source UK Ltd.
Milton Keynes UK
UKRC010928260820
368583UK00027B/221